Trial Run

Anne Metikosh

CRIMSON
ROMANCE

Avon, Massachusetts

This edition published by
Crimson Romance
an imprint of F+W Media, Inc.
10151 Carver Road, Suite 200
Blue Ash, Ohio 45242

www.crimsonromance.com

Dedication

"THE IMPORTANT THING IS THIS: TO BE READY AT ANY MOMENT TO SACRIFICE WHAT YOU ARE FOR WHAT YOU COULD BECOME."—CHARLES DICKENS

CHAPTER ONE

The real turning point in a woman's life is not the day she marries the guy or wins the promotion, it's the morning she decides not to mail a letter, or the afternoon she sits at home and watches the woods fill up with snow.

Or the evening she passes a newsstand where every headline banners the same story.

In varying degrees of outrage, hostility and sensationalism, Tuesday's headlines all reported that John Randall (Randy) Outray III had been arrested on charges of rape and murder.

The Outrays were fixtures in the tabloids. For five generations the local lumber barons had provided as much pulp for the gossip mill as they had for the papermill, their every move gleefully examined at checkout counters and beauty salons across the county. Now they had advanced to the front pages of the dailies. I snatched up copies of the quickly disappearing *Daily Express* and *Dahgue County Barker* and stuck them in my briefcase for when I got home.

I lived in one-fifth of a mansion whose glory days are long past. A couple of years ago a developer bought the property from a Dahgue county doyenne who was eager to trade the castle for capital. The developer had divided the house into five units, which he sold at a substantial profit to investors like me, who aspired to own something unique.

My south-facing corner overlooked what was once the kitchen garden. I still cultivated a few clumps of parsley and basil there, but I'm not much of a cook, so the bulk of my little acreage was devoted to perennials. Every year I divided and transplanted, adding new bulbs and thinning old growth as whim dictated. The result was a satisfying mix of shape and color that I enjoyed year-round from the window whose box seat I have lavished with pillows.

I kicked off my shoes, opened a bottle of red wine and curled up on the seat, making a small ceremony of filling my glass and toasting the air before shaking open the papers.

Randy Outray smiled at me with monied arrogance from page one of the *Dahgue County Barker*. The story was replete with flattering details of his schooling, social, and sporting lives. Center stage was a florid description of the crime he had allegedly committed. At the bail hearing, Randy's statement to inquisitive journalists had been a laconic finger, which the *Barker* published as "no comment" and the *Press* translated into probable guilt.

Not being a graduate of the local college nor a member of The Clubbe, the publisher of the Concord-based *Press* owed nothing to Kingsport Pulp and Paper. Over the caption "Erring Heir," he printed a photo of the Outray clan in deep mourning, acknowledging in the smallest possible typeface that the picture had actually been taken at Grandpa John's funeral the year before. Though presented in less unctuous terms, the family history was again featured on page one. The victims' names were mentioned on page two.

I had never heard of Susan and Tracey Forrester. I had no idea of who they were or where they lived, what they fought or laughed or cried over, but I learned that night in horrific detail exactly how they had died. Their murder was a headline on the radio and a feature on the *News at Six*. In a voice full of pleasurable distress, the solemn, sincere male news anchor promised film at eleven. I wondered fleetingly how that was possible. Did they plan to stage a reenactment, some kind of amateur crime drama, using local thespian talent for the roles of murderer and victims? There was a brief shot of the widower, Ian Forrester, leaving the coroner's office. Commentary still focused on the Outrays; journalists speculated on the defense to be mounted on Randy's behalf. Twenty-four hours after their death, the torn lives and mangled bodies of Susan and Tracey Forrester had already assumed an aura of unreality, as if their pain had disappeared along with the people who suffered it.

CHAPTER TWO

On Wednesday morning, I let myself in to Mel Deloitte's house using the key he had given me. All my clients give me keys. After eight years, it still amazes me, that level of trust. After all, what do they really know about me, apart from the obvious: I'm free, white, and over twenty-one. My business card reads "Nina Ryan, Household Manager" which means that, for a fee, my clients can relax in the knowledge that their bills will be paid on time, their dogs walked, plants watered, houses cleaned, larders stocked, gardens tended, and travel arrangements made.

They know so little about me, and I know so much about all of them.

I don't read diaries but I do read clues. I'm there when the phone rings. I straighten the cards on the mantle; I check for dust behind the headboards; I balance the ledgers. So I know who has half a million socked away in an offshore trust; I know who doesn't sleep with his wife; I know who drinks, who gambles, who beats the dog. I recognize the signs of leaving. If push ever came to shove, I could make a fortune in blackmail.

Deloitte looked startled when I entered his kitchen.

"Oh, hi. You're early."

I shook my head. "You're late. It's eight thirty."

The lawyer glanced at his watch and frowned. "Shit, this damned thing is broken again. Three thousand dollar watch and it's in for repairs more than it's on my wrist. I'll be out of your way in a sec."

"No hurry. Finish your breakfast."

"Listen, do me a favor? Go into my study and bring me the big buff folder on the desk."

Deloitte's study was the only room in the house to escape

his ex-wife's passion for Victorian-era decor. She was long gone, departed in a huff over the philandering that had made her the second Mrs. D in the first place, but hadn't stopped after the ring went on her finger. Deloitte was paying ten thousand a month for that mistake, which he probably considered a bargain. Number One had cost him more, because of the children.

Deloitte liked to keep files on his desk, framed by open volumes of law journals and other learned tomes. He felt the clutter gave him an air of harassed overwork. To me it merely looked untidy but his clients seemed perversely reassured by the disorder. They took it as a sign that their man was indeed a working legal eagle, not a dilettante out to bilk them of their substantial savings. Twenty years ago, the firm of Deloitte, Hoskins, and Gold found a profitable niche among the socially prominent and awfully affluent of Kingsport and Dahgue County. It's astonishing to me how many of them had difficulty keeping their hands out of the till and one another's pants.

The folder Deloitte had sent me to fetch was lying in the middle of the blotter. Loose papers, photocopies, and faxes spilled out the side. Judging from the time and date on the last one, the lawyer had obviously been at work in the wee hours. That was understandable; the name on the tab was Outray.

I went back to the kitchen and handed Deloitte his file. He reached for it with one Bahamas-tanned hand while cramming a piece of toast into his mouth with the other. Not a crumb spilled onto his immaculate silk suit. Despite the late-night bags under his eyes, Deloitte looked like what he was; a successful, mature professional, graying into elegant middle age.

"The marmalade spoils it," I said.

"What?"

"The marmalade on your chin. Doesn't go with the suit."

"Shit," he said. Using the toaster as a mirror, he swiped at his chin with the dishcloth. "Okay, I'm outta here."

"Have a good one."

"Right."

With the Outrays as clients, having a good one was going to be a stretch. According to the news, Randy had been arrested almost as soon as the Forrester's bodies were discovered. There seemed to be no lack of evidence tying him to the crime and, so far, no denial of his involvement. I wondered how his lawyer planned to represent him.

Deloitte's house, like its owner, was high maintenance. The antique armoires and porcelain knickknacks gave a pretty fair indication of his hourly billing rate. A small army of people dusted and vacuumed, cooked and did laundry, washed the car and cut the lawn. I coordinated their efforts. I told them when to polish the silver and checked that none was missing when they were through. I paid the bills and balanced the checkbook, which is how I knew how much he paid his ex-wives and what his dues were at The Clubbe.

The Kingsport Clubbe was exclusive by virtue of both its fees and the self-interest it promotes. By doubling a consonant and adding an "e," The Clubbe had erected the facade of a fitness forum over the reality of a frat house. Well-muscled young men presided over state-of-the-art treadmills and weight machines but the lounges were staffed by nubile "hostesses" who chuckled all the way to the bank over the minor perversions and guilty secrets of Kingsport's rich and famous.

Such duality made me anxious. It reminded me of a geyser, threatening the comfortable green world of the surface with a viscous mass bubbling out of control somewhere below.

CHAPTER THREE

I had an errand to run downtown. I had just spent an hour with two Labrador retrievers and I didn't have time to go home and change before the main post office closed. I gave my sweater a quick swipe with the clothes brush I kept in the car. It only spread the dog hair more evenly. I sighed. My own good grooming would have to wait. I scuttled in under the disapproving gaze of the security guard who had to unlock the door to let me back out. I glanced at my watch. Five past six.

The post office was just around the corner from my sister Kerrin"s office, so I decided to drop in and touch base. Usually, she bore the intrusion politely.

Kerrin's office occupied the ground floor of a two-story house in what used to be a working class neighborhood. The working class couldn't afford to live there anymore because the upwardly mobile had taken it over, aggressively turning houses into condos, offices, and faddish boutiques. Where lovingly tended gardens once bloomed, now stone cobbles lay heavy. A solitary oasis of green persisted at the far end of the block; ten square feet of grass, garnished with a spreading maple tree and a wrought-iron bench.

Kerrin's building stood opposite the green. The brass nameplate on the door read "K. Adams, Trial Consultant." Renovators had sandblasted the dirt-streaked exterior and trimmed the interior with bleached oak and hanging plants. Reproduction watercolors in muted tones hung on the off-white walls. Coordinating fabrics cover chairs and windows, ambient lighting brightened the workspaces. It was almost painfully tidy. There were no scattered files here, no open reference books, no family photos cluttering the desk.

When I walked in, Kerrin's secretary, Louise, was tidying up the office for the night, her angular frame bent to retrieve a piece of paper that had slipped behind the copier. She glanced up as the door snicked shut behind me. Louise is a comfortable fifty-five, with a broad forehead, small nose and determined chin. Behind steel-rimmed glasses, her brown eyes look smaller than they are, which is probably the fault of the lenses. Laugh wrinkles pucker the sides of her mouth, giving her face a homey, lived-in look.

"I like your hair," I said. Corrugated gold waves encased her head like a helmet.

"I know, it looks awful." She made a face. "The best that can be said for it is it will grow out."

"Why gold?" I said.

"It was one of Darlene's experiments." Darlene was Louise's teenaged granddaughter. She dreamed of becoming the next Vidal Sassoon.

I nodded at Kerrin's office. "Is she alone?"

Louise shook her head, waggling her eyebrows suggestively. I peeked around the open door. Mel Deloitte was sitting in the wing chair facing Kerrin's desk.

Fully half of Kingsport's female population harbored a secret passion for Mel Deloitte. Kerrin's secretary nursed a matchmaker's hopes for her boss but Kerrin herself displayed not one iota of interest.

Louise switched off the power bar that fed computer, copier, and fax machine. Without the background hum, Kerrin's voice carried clearly into the outer office.

"Be realistic, Mel, no jury is going to buy self-defense in this case. Your client hit a seventy-five-year-old grandmother. All the sympathy is going to be with the grandmother."

"The woman threatened him with a gun."

"Yes, which turned out to be plastic. It was her grandson's cowboy pistol."

"The kid didn't know that—he thought she was really going to shoot him."

"Mel, you know that's not the point. It doesn't matter what the kid thought, it matters what the jury thinks. And believe me, no jury will think that a six foot, hundred and eighty pound twenty-year old felt seriously threatened by a white-haired granny waving a toy pistol."

Deloitte sighed. "So what am I supposed to do? The truth is, my client decided to have some Saturday night fun robbing the corner grocery, and even though the cashier was a little old lady with a toy gun, he bopped her on the head before he took off with the cash. If I tell that story to the jury, I might just as well send the kid up now."

Kerrin frowned. "Don't you have anything you can use in his defense? History of abuse, mental illness, drug use, even? Something that will get the court on his side, make them see him as a victim, too?"

This was an absurdity that Kerrin had tried, unsuccessfully, to explain to me more than once. It was the job of the defense team to protect the accused, she said. Even if they can't root for him, the trick, and their ethical duty, was not to let their personal feelings interfere with their efforts on his behalf.

"The defense must always try its best for the client."

Over the years, Mel Deloitte had reached the pinnacle of the defense lawyer's art; he could sound as though he believed what he was saying even when he didn't.

My sister, the psychologist-turned-trial-consultant, was another matter. I remember the impassioned arguments she used to mount for the rights of the accused. Her vehemence had shocked my parents but her husband, Brian, had adored her for it. "I put myself in my client's position, entirely," she would say. "I don't think about the victim very much, nor should I."

How many lifetimes ago was that? Dad and Mom were both gone now; Dad mercifully fast of a heart attack, and Mom slowly, in that long series of retreats into silence that left family and friends on the outside, hopelessly searching for the woman who was no longer there. It had seemed right, at the time, to put my life on hold for a while to look after her. Kerrin had been busy with her practice, with

Brian and the baby. But somehow it meant I missed the next logical step in the progression from MBA to CEO, and by the time I was ready to get back in line, the next blow had fallen.

Deloitte was making goodbye noises in Kerrin's office. He paused in the doorway, shaking his head. "I didn't really expect you to support a plea of self-defense here, Kerrin, but it would have been nice, just for once, not to have to jump through hoops trying to come up with an excuse for the inexcusable. Days like this, I wonder why I ever got into criminal defense work in the first place."

I was pretty sure it was the thrill of criminal activity, the titillation of sex and violence, that had him hooked, but I wasn't about to say so.

"Ho, hey there," he said, catching sight of me in the waiting room. "I didn't know you did offices. Kerrin, your cleaning lady's here."

"She's not my cleaning lady. She's my sister."

Deloitte was too well-schooled to register surprise, but I could see the comparisons being drawn. Ten years my elder, Kerrin stood very tall beside me, sleek and quietly composed in her designer suit. My jeans and sweatshirt were rumpled from grooming the Sanderson's dogs, curly hair pulled loosely into a knot on top of my head. They were surface contrasts, but they went personality-deep. Events that had hardened my sister to a narrow focus had left me as blurred as a clumsy photograph. Kerrin had spliced her life back together in patches of black and white. I still floundered in a miasma of gray.

CHAPTER FOUR

Sonja Reid fiddled with the thin silver bracelets encircling her wrist. The faint jangle of metal was her standard preface to small talk and it required no great psychic powers to divine what her topic of the day was likely to be. Everyone in Kingsport was debating the same question.

"I wonder how much it will cost the Outrays to bail Randy out of this one."

A heavy varnish of cosmetics restricted her facial expression but Sonja's tone carried clearly across the room. We were in the library at Reidmore, a pun not intended by the owner of the house, whose sole interest in books lay in color-coordinating their dyed leather spines. Sonja Reid was a twice-anointed pillar of Kingsport society, having been born into one preeminent family and married into another. She was highly regarded by the disenfranchised for her charitable works, though I suspected that for Sonja, doing good had long ago taken the place of feeling good. Her latest pet project was the Youth Development Project and Sonja had gone to considerable effort, and no small expense, to remodel herself in an image suitable to the director of such an enterprise.

I finished tallying the numbers on a bank statement against the ones in Sonja's ledger. Once again, she had neglected to record the checks she had written to cash. She seemed to believe that "pin money" didn't count. Unfortunately, her pins tended to be gold-plated.

Ignoring the slightly malicious bent to her comment on the Outrays, I said, "According to the news, it was two million."

"Oh, I didn't mean it literally, dear." Sonja fingered the bronze chrysanthemums that graced a highly polished drum table. "I meant I wonder just how the family will buy their son's way out of trouble this time. His escapade last year cost them a new library for the college." She put a finger to her lips, so that I would understand the confidential nature of her remark.

I took perverse pleasure in attracting Sonja Reid's condescension because it also attracted her garrulity. In a social circle where gossip could easily transmute to a knife in the back, I made an innocuous sounding board for all the hearsay, rumor, and speculation that Sonja thrives on.

My fortunes derived from members of the monied set with an aversion not only to the hands-on evils of day-to-day life, but also to the underpinnings of lifestyle. Budgets and business correspondence bored them. My peripheral involvement in their lives fed their sense of position. They made me privy to their opinions, but not party to them. Listening, even with half an ear, provided me with a comprehensive mental map of Kingsport, a pin dot reference that plotted the patterns of social commerce that shaped the community.

Sonja prattled on. " . . . Zoe, poor lamb, had to take a month's rest at Bretton Woods. Her doctor insisted. That Randy would try the patience of a saint. And the Lord knows Zoe is hardly a saint. But this! This has to be the absolute worst for the Outrays."

"For the Forresters, too," I said, shutting the ledger and sliding it back into the desk drawer.

"Who, dear?"

"The Forresters. The family of the woman and the little girl who were killed."

"Oh. Yes. Yes, of course. Dreadful for them."

Despite the family's request that funeral services for Susan and Tracey Forrester remain private, Saturday's News at Six had run extensive film of grim-faced pallbearers shouldering their double load. The camera had lingered over-long on the second, pathetically small coffin. Close behind the caskets followed a haggard Ian Forrester and three grief-stricken people who must have been grandparents. Their pain was palpable.

I had flicked off the television and left the papers unread.

Studiously ignoring any psychological implications, I spent Sunday afternoon dressed in my father's ancient khakis and tweed jacket, carefully mounding winter mulch around my roses and planting tulip bulbs in the border.

Sonja was still talking. "Of course, the boy has always been unstable. I suppose that's the tack they'll take."

"Pardon me?"

"The approach they'll use in court, dear. Mel Deloitte will have to say Randy's out of his mind or something and they'll send him for a cure somewhere."

I stared at her blankly.

She made a small "tch" of impatience. "The case is going to trial, dear, didn't you know?" A heavily lacquered nail tapped the newspaper I hadn't read. "Mel Deloitte—such a charming man, do you know him?—made a statement to the press last night. Randy Outray's going to exercise his democratic right to a fair trial." She lowered her voice for effect. "Max told me the DA offered him a deal, but he wouldn't go for it."

Max was Sonja's husband, chairman of the board at Kingsport Pulp and Paper and, unless I missed my guess, another member of The Clubbe. If I were married to Silicone Sonja, I thought uncharitably, I'd join, too.

"Apparently the case against him is pretty much iron-clad—but if he accepts the plea bargain, it means a life sentence. Whereas if he goes to trial, who knows, Mel might actually be able to make a jury think he's innocent or something."

My stomach clenched at the idea of a trial, not because of any fellow feeling I harbored for the Outrays, but because of Kerrin. Mel Deloitte was sure to call on her expertise for a high profile case like this one, because, guilty or not, as long as Randy Outray wanted a trial, his lawyer would need to find some way to defend what he had done.

*

At one o'clock I stopped by Phil's Diner for a quick sandwich before going on to my afternoon job. Several of my clients were half-days and I liked to offset the desk work with a little exercise. Most days, I walked the Sanderson's dogs, two handsome labs, one black, one yellow, both trained as guides for the blind. Guiding was a tough job; a dog's useful life was usually over by age eight. When the dogs retired, they needed to find new homes; canine hierarchy won't allow for a younger dog to take over the responsibilities of the senior one.

Colonel and Mrs. Hugo Sanderson were retired, too. A bullet in Iraq had ended the colonel's part in a diplomatic mission several years ago and confined him to a wheel chair. His wife was still ambulatory, but frail. They could manage staid walks around the neighborhood. They paid me to run Caleb and Kelsey in the ravine. Mrs. Sanderson called it their "little adventure." The amount she was willing to pay to finance the fun had shocked me at first, but according to a segment I watched on *Enterprise*, the Sandersons were not alone in their devotion to their pets. The piece spotlighted a young entrepreneur currently raking in the bucks by offering day care for dogs that costs more than most people spend on their kids. "Coddled Canines" had a six-month waiting list and was about to expand to New York and L.A.

I set off with pooper scoop in hand, Caleb on my left and Kelsey on my right. Both walked slightly in front of me as they had been trained to do, stopping automatically at corners, vying a little with each other over the right to be the leader.

Thanks to a farsighted city planner, Kingsport was blessed with an extensive ravine system that successive mayors have carefully preserved as a screen against the ugliness of the pulp mill. If you entered and left the city by Route 2, and the breeze was stiff enough, you might never know the mill existed.

Maple Key Trail came up out of the ravine a quarter of a mile from the Sanderson house. Usually I followed it around in a five-mile loop, letting the dogs off their leads to snuffle in the underbrush and chase a few squirrels.

The sun felt warm on my back, a fading vestige of summer. Nights were cold enough to leave a faint pattern of frost on scarlet leaves. The fallen ones made a satisfying scrunch underfoot and I couldn't resist kicking up the piles, looking for hibernating bears the way I used to when I was six.

"Bears don't sleep in the leaves," my father had told me. "And besides, it's too early for them to be hibernating."

I kicked the leaves up anyway.

Half-way around the loop, three trails merge and it was at their junction that I spotted the yellow tape. It stretched around a copse of young white birch, the bright color complementing the still-hanging leaves, the words "Crime Scene-Do Not Enter" plainly visible in black. Someone had ignored the warning and crossed the line to place a spray of lilies in the center of the circle. A similar bouquet had graced Susan Forrester's coffin.

Normally the path was deserted, apart from the odd hiker or birder to nod at in passing. Today, half a dozen people had congregated for what I thought at first might be a private pilgrimage. Then I recognized Cindy Maravich from *Talk TV*, complete with cameraman, sound, and lights. I whistled the dogs to me and steered them abruptly onto Woodchuck Way.

Our new path dipped into a hollow and crossed the creek before rising again on the other side, where a scattering of houses backed onto the ravine. I wondered if Susan and Tracey Forrester had lived in one of them. The newspapers said they often walked in the ravine. Perhaps they, too, had kicked through the leaves in a whimsical search for bears. Had there been time for memories of past happiness or regret, or had their terror been all-encompassing? Could the mother think of anything beyond the pain of watching her daughter die? My throat began to ache, an all-too-familiar presage of tears. What possible purpose could be served by such a death? The sense of it was beyond my imagining. Only the flesh and blood of it was real.

CHAPTER FIVE

With one eye on the clock, I grated old cheddar cheese into some macaroni and debated about a drink to go with it. The radio blatted in the background.

"They oughta fry the son of a . . . right now! Save the taxpayer a . . . pot full of money."

Red Reilly's censor button was working overtime. His talk show *Open Line* was a daily feature on Radio Kingsport. It was the vehicle from which he harangued the listening audience, exhorting them to his particular brand of venom. To me he was fascinating, like a deadly snake, and just as frightening. He was a man who made hate easy by making it funny.

"Everyone needs a voice; *Open Line* is yours." Sometimes Red oversaw a general bitch session, but that day the fact that the Outray case was going to trial provided a focus for on-air debate. The first few callers sounded sane enough, upholding everyone's right to a fair trial and approval of the jury system. It was all rather tame until Red stirred it up with his response to a woman I suspected was a shill. She spoke in the long-suffering voice of the professional martyr.

"I have four boys, Red, two of them about the same age as young Randy Outray, and I can understand, as I'm sure other mothers can, how in these fast times, what with all the peer pressure and the drugs, how boys sometimes can act without thinking."

Red barked in astonishment. "Did I hear you right, ma'am? That's your heartfelt reaction to this . . . this heinous crime? A man brutally attacks and callously murders a woman and her four-year old daughter—four years old ma'am, that's how old that little girl was—and then rapes their dead bodies, and you have the nerve to call in here and say to the people of this city that boys sometimes act without thinking? Let me ask you something, ma'am. Are you under medical supervision of any kind?"

The number of deleted expletives rose exponentially after that. It was interesting to note that none of the subsequent callers was anyone the Outrays might consider a peer on any level. Despite an outward show of being "just folks," there was a strict demarcation between the haves and have-nots of Dahgue County, and it seemed implausible that an Outray would accept the judgment of a jury comprised of any of Red Reilly's disciples.

While I dined on macaroni and red wine, I reviewed notes for my lecture. Once a week I taught a class at Metcalf, the local business college.

New Hampshire was overrun with institutes of learning. During the Revolutionary War, our little state spearheaded a movement to produce an intelligentsia more attuned to the philosophies of an emerging nation than an old, established one. Doubts about the success of the venture may have arisen in 1850 when Ralph Metcalf, for whom the business school was named, was elected governor under the auspices of the Know-Nothing Party.

Initially, the trustees at Metcalf were reluctant to hire me. Despite the fact that I hold an advanced degree in business administration, they felt that a household manager was under-qualified to teach at their school. My references finally persuaded them. I ran a very successful small business, with low overhead, high income, and none of the jockeying for position I would have to endure in a large corporation. It was a career I fell into more or less at random. Years of caring for my mother had taught me the finer points of dealing with health professionals, social services, legal consultants and financial advisors, and in all of those areas, I had encountered scores of people, unafflicted by any dementia, who were nonetheless bewildered by the mazes of bureaucracy. Sheer detail overwhelmed them. It occurred to me then that there were bound to be people ready and willing to pay for someone else to shoulder that burden.

I mentioned it to Kerrin once and she surprised me not long after Mom died by referring me to the Sandersons. Business quickly snowballed until I was as busy as I wanted to be, and with as varied and autonomous a working life as I could contrive.

Based on the adage that you don't get rich working for someone else, I designed a course called "Alternatives," in which I explored atypical business opportunities with my students, encouraging them to target needs in the community that their particular skills and interests could fill. I taught them how to draw up a business plan, how to assess the viability of their ideas and determine the practicalities of putting them into effect. Some used my class as a filler, their hearts and minds already dedicated to big business. I've had a few who thought it was a joke and walked out after the first session, but several have been keyed in to new possibilities and one or two have already made successful starts. Lately, I've been toying with my own plans for a permanent "Ideas Center" that would provide assistance to inventors who lacked the know-how to bring their novelties to market. So far, it's just a thought.

I steered my little Subaru into a parking space under one of the floodlights near the main walkway to the college. The lot might be full now, but come ten o'clock it would be nearly empty and the sculptured shrubbery that is so eye-catching by day casts too many shadows for comfort at night.

As usual, there was a line-up at the coffee counter inside Grosvenor Hall. What used to be self-service, pay at the cash register, had upscaled into a three-person operation offering at least a dozen blends of coffee and the now-mandatory cappuccino and caffè latte. I ordered a decaf, black, no sugar and then got a withering look from the well-scrubbed girl behind the counter for selecting a huge, gooey brownie to go with it. It seemed I was crossing some invisible food boundary. Pastry was okay with cappuccino; decaf, no sugar, apparently demanded high-fiber wheat germ.

"Hey, Debbie!" someone called.

I grinned and nodded at the sweatered arm waving me over to join her at a small table. One of my students had laughingly dubbed me Debbie Domestic in honor of my day job. As I stuffed change back into my purse, I glanced at my watch. Ten minutes should see me through the brownie and safely into the classroom.

I slung my knapsack over my shoulder and picked my way around an overturned chair and someone's discarded notes. Newspaper littered the seat I was heading for. I would have dumped it into the recycling box, but my tablemate stopped me.

"I'll take it. I haven't finished reading it yet."

Corey Wayne was completing a degree in interior design. She's was about my age, which means she's on the wrong side of thirty, but where my hair was liberally streaked with premature gray, hers was still glossy black. She figured her adolescent twins will even us up pretty soon. She had married her high school sweetheart right after the prom, driven, I suspected, by impending motherhood. Either luck or love had overcome the odds of failure. Now she and Geoff, a carpenter, were hoping to start up their own decorating business. Given Corey's hectic schedule, I wasn't surprised she didn't have time to get through a newspaper, though the *Barker* really doesn't demand much more than a skim.

DID RANDY REALLY DO IT? was its question of the day.

Predictably, the Outray's paper cast doubt on the guilt of the Outray's son. When interviewed, teachers lauded Randy's scholastic abilities and teammates applauded his athletic ones. They recited a litany of achievement, which, though conspicuously lacking in public service, demonstrated no overtly antisocial behavior. The minutiae of his life were recorded in the *Barker* as though for a Memorable Moments album of the kind doting mothers maintained. One enterprising journalist even noted Randy's medical history, including a broken arm when he was eight, a head injury from a fall when he was twelve, and a cracked ankle skiing in Aspen last year. What bearing any of it had on the murder charge was not explained.

CHAPTER SIX

When I picked up the phone, my caller responded to "hello" with the bald statement, "I need your help" which identified her as readily as a name.

Conversations with Kerrin often began without preamble. I laid on the couch nestled in an ancient yellow afghan, bolstered by a glass of chardonnay. Stacked on the floor beside me were a dozen dog-eared travel magazines. Each one chronicled a journey not taken. When the phone rang, I had to tear myself away from a Montana dude ranch to answer it.

I knew from past experience what my sister wanted and it wasn't personal help, but professional.

"Kerrin, I'm working. I can't . . . "

"Come on. One of my mock jurors let me down at the last minute. I need someone to fill in. Wednesday. Mel'll give you the day off. I already talked to him."

"Nice of you to arrange it," I said drily. As usual, she took no notice.

I had been coerced onto one of Kerrin's mock juries before. I didn't enjoy it. I'm not sure I approve of test-marketing a criminal case before trial. Molding the truth to an acceptable form flew in the face of justice as I understood it.

Ten years ago, my father had been outraged by Kerrin's liberal stance. "Don't tell me you've become one of those bleeding hearts who believe all these young hoodlums are victims, too? The system has somehow let them down, so they're not responsible."

Kerrin's reply had been equally emphatic. "Certainly the system has let them down. D'you know that 99 percent of the injustice associated with crime happens before the principals ever even come into contact with the criminal justice system? Obviously, the victim has already been victimized and, more often than not, the defendant has been subjected to some kind of abuse, too—anything from inadequate prenatal care to exclusion from the work force. The police and the courts and the prisons only come into it later. They're nothing but mop-up operations."

My sister had championed the rights of the accused with all the fervor of a recent convert. A compelling young lawyer named Brian Adams had persuaded her that her degree in psychology could be more profitably employed outside a clinical setting, so Kerrin had become a trial consultant, hired by defense teams to help select jurors and devise case strategies.

It didn't really matter to me then what Kerrin did for a living, as long as she kept bringing Brian Adams home with her. My seventeen-year old heart was broken when the two of them announced their engagement. Even when it mended, I idolized Brian, though our lives barely touched after I left for college.

By the time I finished grad school, Kerrin and Brian were busy professionals with an infant son, Rory. Dad had been dead a year and Mom was starting to fail, mentally, if not physically. I hadn't intended to settle back in Kingsport, but, ultimately, I couldn't ignore my mother's need. I had inherited her ingrained sense of family duty; pride made me indispensable. Victims of Alzheimer's disease tend to die by inches, and the right time to make a break, to commit Mom to a care facility, never seemed to come. I moved back in to my old room and ran my mother's house, and her life, channeling my education and energies into the details of daily existence that had become too much for her to handle. My world narrowed to hers and my only points of light became, not a family of my own, but a husband and son borrowed from my sister.

When he was two, Rory died in a head-on collision with a truck. Brian, who was driving their car, lingered for three days before Kerrin finally allowed them to unplug the life support. Afterward, she went straight back to work, burying herself in other people's grief and gaining a reputation as a hard-ass who always played to win. She hardly seemed to notice when our mother finally died.

My sister's peremptory summons grated. I had spent the last three years meeting her for Friday dinners, persuading her to take in a show, cooking our Christmas turkey. My vigil for my sister hadn't been much different from the one for my mother, and the grace with which I maintained it was wearing thin.

*

Since my cozy evening had already been interrupted, I decided I might as well run some errands. The Towne Market was open twenty-four hours a day. I don't know anyone who shops at three a.m. but I do like to go late in the evening, when most people are glued to the tube. I picked over eggplant, zucchini, and tomatoes, then cruised the aisles for staples. Usually there's no line up at nine o'clock, but when I trundled my buggy to the check out, there were two people waiting impatiently behind a blue-rinsed matron who was giving the clerk a hard time about the price of mayonnaise. According to the flyer, it was on special at $2.39. The clerk had rung it through at $2.69. The customer was indignant over the error, unhappy with the clerk's attitude, and demanded to speak to the manager. It was the sort of diplomatic crisis that could take a while to sort out. Naturally, there were no other clerks available.

Marketing minds must have had just such a scenario in mind when they set up magazine racks by the cashier and stocked them with tabloids. What better to do while waiting to spend money than pick one up? It was impossible not to be beguiled by the tantalizing covers. This week's teaser was a grainy reproduction of an old centerfold, the usual shot of a nubile body coyly shrouded in satin sheets. A bland, pretty face smiled seductively into the camera. The girl in the photo looked about nineteen. I had seen her face often in the last few weeks, in the newspapers and on television. The girl was Susan Forrester.

CHAPTER SEVEN

Personality had quickly become the salient feature of the Outray case, the public being less fascinated by the murders themselves than by who was involved. The eight mock jurors assembled in Kerrin's office were no exception.

As a trial consultant and advisor on jury selection, Kerrin was not interested in the foibles of individual personality; what she wanted in a mock juror was a representative of a particular segment of society. She purposely sought out types. By analyzing a juror's response to the case being presented, Kerrin could determine with reasonable accuracy the feelings and opinions of like-minded members of the community, and she would try to stack the real jury accordingly. Over the years, Kerrin had built an extensive network of acquaintances and referrals from whom she constructed her mock juries. She pooled them from every walk of life and every social sphere, and she treated each of them with the same benign indifference. Some were truly interested in the process; some felt a measure of civic responsibility that they could fulfill more expediently in a couple of afternoons in Kerrin's office than in several weeks in a courtroom; some were simply curious or in need of the fee that Kerrin paid. Apart from me, all were there voluntarily.

I surveyed the group assembled in the conference room and thought that, as a random market sample, Kerrin had done quite well. We were an eclectic mix, males outnumbering females five to three.

Two of the men had obviously dressed down for the day, but the tasseled loafers and Ralph Lauren shirts couldn't disguise their Phi Beta Kappa arrogance. There was probably a twenty-five-year age difference between them but the mold had remained intact and I wondered if their opinions, too, would bridge the generation gap.

The older one claimed the head of the table; the younger slid into the chair at his right. The rest of us settled into whatever seat was nearest. A coffee pot lent focus to the table and people began to make little busy motions with spoons and mugs. Louise removed the pot for refill. Her hair was less rigidly fixed to her head today, though still determinedly blonde. Kerrin glossed over introductions.

"I'm not a lawyer," she said. "And you're not a real jury. It's their job, the job of the defense and the jurors, to try this case in court. They deal with the law. I'm here—we're here—for the human element. I want to learn what convinces you. What you believe. What turns you on, what turns you off. Okay?" Several heads bobbed. "It's okay for you to have opinions and feelings. That's what you're here for." Kerrin looked directly at me. "It's not okay to not share them."

I considered the faces ranged around the table and thought I could make a pretty fair estimate of the feelings they would express. An English professor once told me that there are only seven basic story lines in all of literature and a like number of stock characters. Individuals may appear to be unique but, in my experience, stereotypes are as common on the streets of Kingsport as in the pages of any novel.

Perched directly opposite the Phi Beta Kappas was a young man with a mild overbite and a tendency to preface each breathy comment with a little shrug. When Kerrin said *okay*, his head bobbed agreement on a neck that looked too fragile to support it.

As far from him as possible slouched a middle-aged man with a doughy face under a bowl of brown hair. The name "Jerry" was stitched in royal blue across the pocket of his pink shirt. On Jerry's right sat a blonde with a fly-catcher hairdo and improbably long, fuchsia nails. She was openly appraising the ensemble worn by the impeccably tailored matron on my left. The simple wool dress under scrutiny couldn't have cost much more than six hundred dollars, which may have been walking around money for Juror #3, but I suspected #7 would have to wait for the knockoffs at Lucy's Labels.

The remaining male juror had settled quietly in the chair on my right. Unlike the others, he was unaccountably difficult to categorize and I eyed him covertly while I tried to find the right label to apply. I guessed his age at about thirty-five, though it was difficult to be sure since a full beard obscured much of his face. I was pleased to note it was the genuine well-trimmed article, a far cry from the scruffy patches currently in vogue. A ray of lines around blue eyes hinted at a sense of humor or a squint.

Taking a fresh pot of coffee from Louise, Kerrin shut the door of the conference room and got down to business.

"I'm sure you are all aware of the Randy Outray case."

Little murmurs of assent were punctuated by a snort from Jerry.

Kerrin said, "Talk to me about it."

Juror #7 waggled pink nails and identified herself as Lila. "Are we supposed to have an opinion already? Because, I mean, we haven't heard any evidence or anything yet and it doesn't seem right to me that we should make an opinion already."

Jerry rolled his eyes. "Like none of us have kept up with the news or nothin'. Don't you read the papers? Or watch TV? Jeez Louise, the whole world knows about this case. What kinda evidence are you lookin' for?"

Lila stiffened. "I don't think we should make up our minds based on hearsay, is all I'm saying." She emphasized the word "hearsay", proud to be able to use it in a sentence.

PBK Senior cleared his throat and waited for attention to focus on him. "If I may, I think what Ms. Adams is trying to establish here, is a framework on which to build. She is not asking for any judgment calls at this point. Am I right, Ms. Adams?"

"Kerrin. Actually Mr. Lyons—Thomas, isn't it?—judgment calls are exactly what I'm after." Lyons subsided with bad grace as Kerrin continued, "This is a very high profile case. It's had lots of media attention and it will have a lot more, all the way through the trial. The jury that will be asked to decide the case will be composed of members of the community just like you people. They'll take an oath to listen impartially to the evidence presented and to try their best to render a fair judgment, but each of them will have opinions just like you do, shaped by emotions and experiences that may not have any bearing whatsoever on the case itself. That's the human side of the justice system and that's why we're here today. To see if we can get a handle on people's opinions."

PBK Junior steepled his fingers and said, "Fascinating."

I was tempted to flash a four-finger vee and say, "Live long and prosper," but I suspected *Star Trek* reruns weren't on his TV viewing list.

My neighbor murmured, "Beam me up, Scotty," the movement of his lips scarcely visible through his beard. I grinned. He winked and held out his hand. "David Maitland."

"Nina Ryan."

The gesture set off a spate of handshakes and introductions that further identified PBK junior as Chad Taylor and the lady in wool as Daintry Gregg. In a breathless rush, the slight young man introduced himself as Brent William.

"Brent William what?" Lila wanted to know.

"Nothing. Just Brent William."

"Really? I've never heard of that before as a last name. Just plain, I mean. I always thought it had an 'ess' on the end, you know, like Williams."

Brent looked bewildered. He seemed rather ingenuous for a young man of twenty-odd. If Kerrin intended him to represent Randy Outray's contemporaries, I thought she had blundered. His naïveté was the complete antithesis of Randy's slick veneer.

CHAPTER EIGHT

In the spring, local TV station WKPT had broadcast a special called *Founding Fathers*. To celebrate Kingsport's two hundred and fifty years of history, the producers mounted a lavish tribute to the visionaries who had hacked fortunes out of New Hampshire's pine forests. Nineteenth century shipbuilding had given way in the early twentieth century to textiles and, more recently, to high-tech communications, but the lumber barons of old lived on in successive generations of Outrays, Reids, and D'Arcys. The final fifteen minutes of the show presented some of the new growth to the populace. Kerrin ran the segment that mattered to us.

Randy Outray had been interviewed in his living room. He occupied his own wing of the family mansion and his decorating style ran to large and electronic. A massive screen flanked by equally impressive speakers dominated one end of the room. There was no conversational grouping; chrome and leather furniture was arranged for maximum screen visibility.

Throughout the interview, the scion of the Outray family lounged across a vast tan sofa, fingers laced around one bent knee, body slightly arched in presentation of self, like a model in a magazine ad. He stared directly into the camera, sparing a glance for the host only when a question was asked. Though he sounded pleasant enough, something in the set of his mouth spoke of a temper too often given rein. Regular features were enhanced by expensive grooming and extensive orthodontics but an enigmatic expression and hooded eyes gave his face an oddly shuttered look. I had the feeling that in a social context he would be discomfiting to know, the predator who subtly invades your spatial comfort zone.

"Well, I don't see how that young man could possibly have done such a terrible thing," said Daintry Gregg. She had the kind of cut-glass accent that belongs in English drawing rooms. "I know his mother. I served with her on the hospital board some years ago."

"You know Mrs. Outray, so therefore her son can't be a murderer?" Jerry said. "That doesn't make sense. Besides, I didn't think there was any question of his guilt. I understood he made a confession."

Kerrin said, "He made a statement, yes."

"Well, I don't get it," Lila said. "If the guy's already confessed, what are we doing here?"

Thomas Lyons spoke with exaggerated patience. "In a criminal case, the United States Constitution guarantees every citizen the right to a jury trial."

"Or in any civil suit exceeding twenty dollars," appended Chad. Like Frick and Frack, these two had already fallen into the habit of completing each other's thoughts. It was an interesting phenomenon, especially as they appeared to have met for the first time here today.

David Maitland said quietly, "A verdict by a representative jury is especially important in a controversial trial like this one—it increases the legitimacy of the process in the eyes of the public."

I looked at him curiously. His expression was impossible to read.

Kerrin said, "There is a plea bargain on the table. The problem is Randy doesn't want to accept it. He wants to go to trial. He feels that if his defense team fights hard enough for him, he'll go home."

"On what grounds do you plan to defend his case?" David asked. "Self-defense?"

Sarcasm was lost on Lila. "No way," she said.

"No way for self-defense?" Kerrin quickly picked her up. "Not possible?"

"You gotta be kidding, lady." Jerry was outraged. "This guy had a knife. He attacked and killed a woman and her little girl and then he raped them, supposedly."

"It must have been the other way around, surely," said Daintry Gregg, as though even the most antisocial act must conform to some kind of social norm.

Kerrin said, "The rapes did occur afterwards. Anybody know what that's called? Necrophilia. Having sex with a dead person. Let me ask you something. How many sane neighbors and friends do you have who go around killing women and children and then proceed to have sexual intercourse with the bodies? Raise your hand if know any. Why not? What happened here?"

Chad shrugged. "He lost it."

"He lost it," Kerrin repeated, enunciating each word clearly. "There is a medical condition, one that is very, very rare—I think there are only two or three documented cases—called pathological intoxication. Two of the symptoms are superhuman strength and necrophilia."

She scanned each face for a reaction, testing the limits of believability for her suggestion. This was the crux of her job, presenting ideas, searching out the theme that would have the widest latitude of acceptance among the jurors.

"Well?" she said. "Is it a defense? Does it work for you? Give me a verdict."

Lila said again, "I don't get it. Patho-whatever intoxication? You mean like he was drunk, at ten o'clock in the morning?"

"No," said Brent, adding in a rush, "I think she means he had, like, repressed desires that, maybe, came out all of a sudden at that time and he said 'to hell with it, I'm going to just act out what I feel I want to do.'" He sagged, deflating like a balloon as air and words ran out together. Jerry smirked openly at the thought of the repressed desires that Brent's willowy figure suggested.

"What a load of crap," he said.

"Is that an established medical condition?" Thomas Lyons demanded. "Are you going to get some kind of doctor to testify that it really exists? Because, frankly, I find it difficult to swallow."

Chad agreed. "It would be easier to accept alcoholic stupor

or something drug-induced. Though I have heard of guys losing it over a truly foxy chick and from what I saw in the papers that Susan Forrester certainly qualified."

"You rotten pig!" Lila spat. "So what if the girl posed for Playboy eight years ago? That gives some guy the right to jump her? And kill her kid?"

Kerrin didn't interfere. I could see her mentally cataloguing the different responses, grading the credibility of the pathological intoxication argument, assessing points of contention. If a single convincing argument could not be found, it might benefit the defense to divide the jurors along just such sexual lines as Lila and Chad were drawing. A hung jury might not be the best case scenario for Randy Outray, but neither would it be the worst.

CHAPTER NINE

"Are you not planning to participate at all?" Kerrin said.

She had allowed us a one-hour break for lunch. The group had scattered to various eateries in the neighborhood, among them a soup and sandwich counter, a deli bar specializing in alfalfa sprouts, and a linen-service restaurant. I had made a detour to the washroom. Kerrin was there, combing out her hair before dampening the ends and coiling them back up into the French twist she habitually wore.

I watched her in the mirror. "I'm waiting for you to get serious," I said.

"What d'you mean?"

"That pathological intoxication stuff was, to quote Jerry, crap. You have no more intention of selling that to Mel Deloitte than I have of flying to the moon."

Kerrin ignored my tone and carefully inserted a comb to hold her hair in place. "It's part of my strategy," she said, "To get these people riled up a bit first, so I get some honest feedback from them. The prosecutor's going to play to the jury's emotions just as hard as Mel is when this thing gets going. You've seen it before, you know both sides choreograph their movements and their words to maximize dramatic impact in the courtroom. It's my job to find out what movements will get the response we're looking for."

Her eyes met mine in the mirror.

"Do you never worry about manipulating the system, Kerrin?"

The challenge surprised her. She crumpled the paper towel in a tight fist and flung it into the bin. "What I'm doing is providing a service to a defendant. Without that service, that leveling of the playing field, justice for the accused is a crapshoot." She spoke with bitter irony. "We may have to accept the mercies of fate over a lot of things but criminal justice, at least, ought to be something more than simply a roll of the dice, don't you think?"

She turned on her heel and yanked open the door to the hall. I followed like a well-trained puppy, anxious for approval after giving offense.

In three years, this was the best we had achieved. Our conversations tended to skate past moral issues, avoiding the depths like a novice afraid to strike out from the safety of shore to the more exposed, but potentially perilous, ice further out. We bore our separate grief with whatever dignity we could muster, burying pain as we had buried our family. I didn't have the courage to continue the encounter and as always, sought refuge in the trivial.

"Lunch?"

Kerrin shook her head. "Louise left a sandwich in my office. I have a few things to do before the others come back."

I wandered out of the building, feeling anxious and unsettled, unsure of my destination. At this point, I only had forty-five minutes left, which let Ristorante Tarina out. Since alfalfa sprouts have never held much appeal, I headed for the hearty comforts of the Sandwich Board, finding when I got there that the only available stool had a broken swivel top. Lunch would have to be take-out, I thought resignedly, until someone said, "Share my booth?"

I recognized the voice immediately, which surprised me, because I had heard it for the first time just that morning. It held an underlying note I couldn't quite define but which gave the impression of someone casually and good-temperedly on terms with life. It is an accent rare among the pompous, rarer still among the self-pitying, and I found it infinitely attractive. David Maitland offered me the extra seat in his booth with a small gesture of welcome.

"Rumor has it the tuna salad is the fastest, but I'm here to tell you that the hamburger is worth the wait."

"It looks it," I said, eyeing a small mountain of beef stacked with tomato, onions, and hot peppers. "The question is, can anyone eat that and not suffer the heartbreak of heartburn afterward?"

"Ah, now there is something only the daring can answer. Are you daring?"

"Not very."

"How 'bout if I buy you a beer to quench the fires?" A pattern of water rings on the table in front of him marked the recent passing of a pilsner glass.

"Make it white wine and I'll accept."

The waitress who drifted over to take my order focused so intently on my mouth that I wondered for a moment if she was hearing-impaired. Though I have often been complimented on my smile, I didn't really think the lipstick I was wearing should excite that much interest. When "Hello, my name is Tara" turned her appraising eyes on the rest of me, I decided she was not so much fascinated as rude. Bad manners have a way of attracting the same; her impudent scrutiny provoked me to examine her just as closely, and I felt David Maitland's gaze sharpen into amusement at the circling of the dogs. I suspected that Tara had been making time with him before I arrived and it was clear that she considered me an unworthy rival. I noted that she had applied her own lipstick far too liberally, inking in contours that nature hadn't given her. Her figure, too, had been adjusted to startling proportions by a French, a very French, half-cup bra. I saw her glance slide momentarily to my own lesser endowments. David saw it, too, and I felt myself color faintly.

"Not to worry," he said blandly, as Tara finally moved away.

"Gee, thanks, Dad."

He grinned, a gesture that instantly transformed him from inscrutable to teddy bear cuddly. I controlled an unexpected urge to snuggle up beside him.

We talked nothings for a while and David ordered the house

specialty, apple crumble, to keep me company while I waded through my burger.

"There's a shaker of chilis here, if you want to liven that up a bit," he said, laughing at the tears the hot peppers had already produced.

"Are you out of your mind?"

"No." He paused. His manner was casual, even abstracted. Then he said, "Do you think Randy Outray is?"

The sudden shift in conversation threw me and I felt obscurely disappointed to be brought back to the subject at hand. "What?"

"Randy Outray. Do you think he's insane?"

I dabbed at streaming eyes with my napkin. "How would I know?"

"How would anyone? But what other defense could there possibly be for what he did?"

I shook my head, gulping half a glass of wine to dampen the fire in my mouth.

"There is precedent for it, you know," he went on. "Remember John Hinckley? They had a videotape of him shooting President Reagan—played it over and over on nationwide TV. When the trial began, no one seriously thought the insanity plea would work, but in the end it did. They said he was schizophrenic."

"Yes," I said slowly, "But wasn't the Hinckley case the exception to prove the rule? Juries aren't usually very receptive to the insanity defense, are they?"

"Aren't they? What about Mark David Chapman?"

"The man who shot John Lennon."

David nodded. "I think a lot of jurors balk at the death penalty. An insanity plea gives them a way to find someone guilty and then punish him by getting him treatment."

His tone should have clued me in, but it didn't. I finished my burger and we walked back to Kerrin's office.

CHAPTER TEN

"We're going to look at some photographs," Kerrin said. She opened a manila envelope and withdrew half a dozen pictures, which she placed one at a time on the table in front of us. "Tell me what you see."

"A bloody knife," Chad said.

"A very bloody knife," amended Jerry, sliding the picture across the table. Daintry Gregg visibly withdrew, as though touching the photograph might mean touching the murder weapon itself. Her lips tightened over a picture of Tracey Forrester holding up a ginger kitten and waving its paw to the camera. It was a blowup of a shot that had appeared in the *Press* the day the little girl was buried.

A professional portrait of Susan Forrester drew a low whistle from Chad. It appeared to have been taken at a glamour studio, one where cosmeticians pay close attention to the sitter's hair and makeup. Something black was draped low around Susan's shoulders, underscoring a pale beauty more refined than in the days of the centerfold.

My stomach clenched at the sight of the mother and child who had been so unsuspecting of what awaited them in the woods. As so often, I thought of Brian and Rory, who had been equally unaware as they tooled along the highway that fine summer evening. The Beach Boys were cranked up on the stereo, the tape somehow surviving amid the wreckage of the car. For weeks, Brian had been teaching Rory the words to "Sloop John B." The little boy loved to mime the action as his father belted out the refrain, pulling on make-believe ropes as he hoisted an invisible sail.

We were told they wouldn't have seen it coming. The tire that spun from the logging truck to smash through their windshield would have been moving too fast.

There had been little enough left of Rory. I had identified him only by a scar on one foot and the tattered cowboy shirt he had been wearing. Kerrin couldn't leave Brian to go to the morgue and, in any event, the doctor had advised against her seeing her mangled child.

Without meeting her eye, I handed the photographs of the Forresters back to Kerrin.

The remaining shots were of the crime scene. People glanced at them quickly and passed them along.

"Gruesome," said Chad.

"They look so vulnerable."

A faint humming began to fill the room, one of those sounds with no translation in human speech that starts low in the back of the throat and issues from the lips as a moan of pain, or a scream. Heads swiveled to stare at Daintry Gregg, who sat hunched in her seat, oblivious to all but her own thoughts. Abruptly she stood up, knocking over her chair in her clumsy haste to escape the room. I noticed a fine tremor in David Maitland's hands as he moved to set the chair back upright.

Kerrin signaled to Louise, then turned back into the room. We all looked at her expectantly. With no change in expression, she said, "Gruesome, okay. Vulnerable. What else?"

There was an interval before someone said, "Butchered."

"The word compassion doesn't even enter in when you look at those pictures."

At his end of the table, Brent murmured, "Aberration."

Kerrin picked up on it quickly. "Does that word come to anybody else's mind? Insane? How many say a person has to be insane to cut two people up like that? Insane to have sex with their dead bodies?"

"Fuck-in' loo-ny tunes," said Jerry. "No question."

*

When the rest of the group disbanded for the day, Kerrin motioned me to linger. I half-hoped David might make the offer of another drink, but once the session was over, he departed with almost ungracious speed. Daintry Gregg had never returned. Shortly after three, Louise had delivered tea to the conference room along with the message that Daintry had resigned her position. Louise had found her in the washroom, draped over the toilet bowl. She offered to call a doctor, but Daintry refused, insisting instead on a cab to take her home. She would leave her Mercedes in the lot until someone could be sent to fetch it.

As soon as the door closed on the last juror, Kerrin was on the phone to Mel Deloitte. With a flick of her hand, she motioned me to the wing chair by her desk. I kicked off my shoes and curled up into it, feet tucked protectively under me, arms wrapped around my knees.

"I'm not sure," Kerrin was saying, "That they can hear anything I say once they look at the photographs."

Mel's swooping baritone rumbled at the other end of the line, a startling counterpoint to Kerrin's uninflected accent.

"Mel, we can't change the facts. The facts are there. So are the pictures. And the prosecution's going to use them. We've got to live with that."

She listened for a moment.

"One for sure, maybe two, figure he has to be a nutbar. The rest were too distressed at the sight of the victims to even spare a thought for him. One woman, who started out leaning to our side, totally lost it. She won't be back. What we need to do now is identify which people will at least listen to us once they've seen those pictures."

Kerrin cradled the receiver and made one or two notes on the pad in front of her. Then she leaned back in her chair, surveying me with her arms folded across her chest, in much the same way that our mother used to signal a showdown. The gauntlet had been thrown in the washroom at lunchtime. It was too late to wish it back. Kerrin and I sat poised on the edge of a confrontation that had nothing to do with the Outray case and everything to do with the unpalatable mixture of guilt and resentment that had strained our relationship to the breaking point. I silently willed the moment away. We had lost everything else. Must we lose each other as well?

I hugged my knees to my chest in a defensive posture that had become habitual and tried an obvious sidestep. "Since you're going to have to find a replacement for Daintry anyway, why not make it two?"

Kerrin refused to be deflected. "No. It's time we had this out." Her words were measured, her voice a curious and strangely comforting blend of psychologist and big sister. "I saw the look on your face while those photos were being passed around. You were thinking about Brian and Rory, weren't you?"

"Yes." I raised my head to look at her. "Yes, I was. Weren't you?"

"No."

Kerrin's answer was as composed as her features. I studied her carefully. Loss had hardened her lovely face, erasing from it something fundamental that I remembered there. Three years into unremitting ache, I still searched for it but, like Winnie the Pooh, the more I looked for it, the more it wasn't there. We never spoke of Brian or Rory, or even of our parents. Until now, their lives, and our lives with them, had been a chapter closed to us both.

"What is it you want from me, Nina?" Kerrin said. "Should I light an eternal flame? Become a professional widow?"

I tried to frame a response but she overrode me, moving with the ease of long practice from defense to attack. "Look at you. Thirty-two years old and you exist like a cloistered nun, floating on the edge of other people's lives. For three years, you've devoted yourself to nurturing me. You think if you hover over me like some kind of ministering angel, making sure I eat properly and don't forget the stockings at Christmas, that things will be . . . restored. That I will be restored."

I hugged my knees tighter. Rigid self-control made my voice colorless almost to the point of stupidity. "That's not fair."

Kerrin said wearily, "Life isn't fair. Just ask me. So what? You endure what you must and thank God it's not worse."

I stared at her, appalled. "Worse? How could it possibly be any worse? They're dead!"

Kerrin drew a long breath, twisting her wedding ring around and around on her finger. It seemed to fit much looser than it used to, dropping to her first knuckle when she moved her hand. She spoke very quietly and carefully, as though addressing someone of limited intelligence. "That's right. Brian and Rory are dead. Whether by accident or as part of some grand design, I don't know. I haven't asked God for explanations lately; I've never believed he sees justice quite the same way we do anyway. I only know I can't live my life bemoaning fate." Kerrin's eyes were bright with unshed tears. "Brian and Rory are dead and here am I, still alive and kicking, and glad, yes, glad," she said fiercely, "That my husband isn't lying like some vegetable in a hospital, glad that my son didn't suffer when he died." She stopped playing with her ring. "Glad that I'm still alive." Her face showed no expression, but her eyes pleaded for acceptance.

I stared at her. I had never understood before then that my sister was a Stoic. Somehow it widened the gap between us. Anger as powerful as pain twisted in my gut. I said bitterly, "Kerrin Adams, a parable for our time." The words echoed like a slap in the quiet room.

Kerrin recoiled as if I had indeed hit her.

Gathering dusk spilled through the window, obscuring the details of the room. In the half-light, my sister's face looked hard as stone, and as strange.

Silence stretched. The moment hung suspended, like a wave before it breaks.

Then Kerrin said, "I'm sorry, Nini," and the wave washed over me, the salt drops tingling and smarting in my eyes at her use of the childhood endearment. "I'm sorry, but I can't help the way I feel. Things happen, and life goes on, and you change, and you can't go back. You have to live it the way it comes."

She was sitting very still behind her desk. Was it a trick of the light or was my sister really a very long way away from me, a lonely figure in the near darkness?

It came to me suddenly that this was how I would always remember her; a woman alone. And I think, for the first time, I began to see her as she really was—not any more as a projection of my adolescent romantic fantasies, the young wife so cruelly widowed, the bereaved and heartbroken mother . . . this was Kerrin, who had been a determined fighter from our earliest days of schoolyard bullies. She had made a career of redeeming the socially unredeemable and she had borne devastating loss with a strength that I, wrapped up in my own crippling despair, had not recognized. We had hoed the same painful row; I, it now seemed, for the more bitter harvest. Kerrin had managed acceptance of what was left to her. It was I who had not.

They say that moments of self-revelation come to everyone. I wonder if they are ever pleasant.

CHAPTER ELEVEN

I drove home along River Road, a route that took me past Oenophile, the wine store. It was Brian who had insisted on educating my palate. Once a week, he would drop by the house with a new label and we would sit at the kitchen table sipping it while Mom slept upstairs or wandered the house like a tribeless nomad. In those days of being caregiver to my mother, Brian was my touchstone and my link with the world beyond 240 Woolner Street.

I had kept very few pieces of furniture from my parent's home but the old pine harvest table was one and I often sat running my fingers over its scarred surface, reading my family history in its dents and scratches. There was the dent from when Dad, in the guise of home-handyman, dropped his hammer; there I had tried to carve my initials with a butter knife; over there, was the burn mark from the cigarette Kerrin had flipped under a cup to avoid my mother's wrath. In the year before she died, Mom had perched at the head of this table for hours on end, a soft rag that had probably been one of our diapers in one hand and a silver teapot in the other. Her body curved protectively over it, she had buffed her reflection in its shiny contours with mindless intensity, as if polishing hard enough could restore her lost personality. The teapot, too, was among the things I had moved from my parents' home to my own. It was stored now in the back of a cupboard, tightly swaddled and slowly tarnishing.

Three years ago, I had been sitting at the table drinking tea when a knock came at the door. I had jumped up eagerly, thinking it might be Brian.

It had been a policewoman.

"Mrs. Ryan?" she had said.

"That's my mother," I told her.

"Miss Ryan, then. Ms. Ryan. Nina? I'm Officer Soames."

I had known it then. The bad news was there, in the piling up of names and Officer Soames's reluctance to settle on one. Brian would never come again to sit with me at this table, to toast me with his wine glass or smile the slow, seductive smile that made me long to reach out and touch the golden hairs on the back of his hand. Rory would never again climb onto my lap, grinning with the jam-smeared satisfaction of a peanut butter feast.

Anguish was socially unacceptable. It was particularly inappropriate when you were young and pretty and it was not your husband and child who were dead, but only your brother-in-law and your nephew. Standing over their graves, it was unseemly to rend your clothes and tear your hair. It was your duty to put grief aside, offer solace to your sister, and return to caring for a mother who no longer knew you.

Somewhere in the house, a tap dripped, a small maddening sound, like a note struck on a piano that is a little out of tune. I poured myself another glass of wine.

My entire adult life had been bound up in the care of others. In the name of duty I had abandoned both career and courtship. Now my mother was dead and my sister had outgrown me. I felt like a novice sailor, alone in a small boat cast suddenly adrift. If I was not to founder, I would need more ballast to balance the sudden weight of a freedom I no longer knew how to exercise.

My maudlin self-analysis was interrupted by the phone. For the first two rings, I debated answering it at all. On the third, I put down my glass and pushed my chair back from the table. By the fourth, I was halfway across the room and I picked up on the fifth, just as voicemail took over. Sonja Reid's voice fluted impatiently over the line.

"I was afraid you might not be there, it took you so long to answer."

"You could have left a message," I said mildly, wishing I hadn't picked up after all. A month ago, I had taken on a project for

Sonja that was turning out to be far more hassle than it was worth.

"I hate leaving messages. I always sound like Betty Boop. Anyway, I don't have to now, as you're there."

"No," I agreed.

"I thought I'd touch base with you regarding the Ball."

Every winter, Max and Sonja Reid host the premier social event of the season, which everyone but Sonja simply calls The Party. It is always held on the Saturday before Christmas, and Kingsport's lesser lights entertain before and after in the reflected glow of its glittering festivity. This year, Sonja was paying me an exorbitant sum to organize the particulars of the Reidmore Winter Ball. She had assembled the guest list and designed the menu herself; it was my job to deploy the caterers, musicians, and decorators necessary to realize her dream. Although I had them all well enough in hand, Sonja was in a constant dither about one detail or another of the arrangements. Tonight, though, she surprised me by asking, not about lobster patties, but about my own attendance.

"You'll have to be there anyway, of course, to oversee things, but Max and I would like you to feel you are our guest as well."

I felt obscurely gratified to be considered, for this occasion at least, to be above the salt, but pleasurable anticipation was laced with sudden worry about what to wear. My wardrobe included none of the Ralph Laurens or Alexander McQueens with which the Reid ballroom would undoubtedly be crowded and I was Scottish enough where my wallet was concerned to be unwilling to purchase one for the occasion. I reviewed what my closet had to offer, rejecting out of hand the tailored suit and plain black dress suitable for weddings and funerals.

Shifting hangers to one side, I reached for the garment bag tucked shyly in behind and unzipping it, lifted out a sheath of midnight-blue velvet, cut high at the neck, plunging low in the back. Though the length might demand altering to current vogue, I felt a smug satisfaction at the way the fabric still clung in all the right places and at the shape of the leg revealed by the skirt. The fine seams, stitched by my mother's clever hand, showed no sign of wear. She had presented me with the dress when I was twenty-three and invited to a dinner dance at the country club. With its simple lines and lovely drapery, I had thought it the most beautiful dress I had ever seen. Nine years later, in the lamplit glow of my bedroom, I caught a fleeting glimpse of the girl who had worn it last. There had been a corsage to grace it then, heart-shaped leaves supporting fragile white blossoms that were veined with cream on throat and wing. The man who had given the flowers had not been my first romance but, as things transpired, he had been my last. Kerrin's barbed comment about cloisters and nuns had been accurately, if painfully, placed.

In love, as in anything else, timing was everything, and in missing a step to care for my mother, I had fallen out of the rhythm of the mating dance. I hadn't minded at first, had even found it satisfying to disappoint the people who said I would not be able to cope with my mother's needs. I hadn't grudged her the unending care; I was very fond of her. But eventually, the feeling that I had built an emotional snare for myself ate away the early contentment I had found in providing for her. Servitude became a habit of mind. It was a natural progression when she died, to make a career out of minding the details of other people's lives and to spend all my emotional capital on my sister. For many years, my self-imposed isolation had seemed safe, and secure. Only lately had it begun to feel like a trap.

Imagination conjured a misty vision of me waltzing with a phantom lover in a ballroom the size of Buckingham Palace while somewhere an orchestra played Strauss. Firmly, I thrust whimsy aside. No simple invitation to a ball was likely to transform this housekeeper into Cinderella.

CHAPTER TWELVE

As November drizzled into December, three topics comprised the local buzz: the weather, which continued cool and rainy long past time for change; the Reidmore Ball, which sent a dozen local businesses smiling to the bank; and the impending trial of Randy Outray. His case was scheduled to be heard early in the New Year, the speed ostensibly to obviate media involvement that might be prejudicial to the defendant. In fact, the lead-up to the trial had already become an integral part of the news. Talking heads debated everything from the jury selection process and the choice of legal counsel for both sides, to possible arguments and likely ramifications. The case would be decided in the public mind before it ever got to court. JusticeTV promised gavel to gavel coverage. Since the days of the O.J. Simpson trial, network producers had salivated whenever a high profile case like this one emerged; ratings always skyrocketed in direct proportion to screen time. Viewers gleefully ingested a continuous stream of info-babble sandwiched between dog food commercials.

The principals in the case had already been transformed into larger than life characters. The defendant with the million-dollar smile was now known as "Dandy Randy, the Angel of Death." Magazines spawned articles on "the Angel and The Centerfold," trivializing the life and death of the two victims and turning a particularly vicious crime into an entertainment.

Since the day after the first mock jury session in Kerrin's office, such representatives of the media as were controlled by the Outray millions had issued broad hints of the defendant's mental instability. An unnamed physician "close to the family" confided to the *Barker* that, as a result of a head injury, Randy suffered from something called a disconnected social response mechanism.

Immediately following this disclosure, WKPT aired a special, featuring interviews with noted psychiatrists and legal experts.

"The insanity defense is an integral part of our legal system," one criminal specialist explained. "The entire system is predicated on the assumption that we exercise free will in our actions and thus can be held accountable for them."

His colleague added sagely, "In law, the assignment of criminal responsibility requires not only that we commit a criminal act, but also that we intend to commit that act. Individuals without a guilty mind or criminal intent are usually not held accountable for their actions."

"Can you give us an example?" the interviewer asked.

"Certainly. Say someone robs a bank because someone else is holding a gun to his head—that person is not accountable for his . . . ," he winked at the camera, " . . . or her, actions. By the same token, someone who runs over a child that darts out in front of his car is not held criminally liable the way someone would be who deliberately aims his car at another person."

The psychiatrist on the panel spoke up earnestly. "According to the American Law Institute, an individual is not responsible for criminal conduct if, at the time and as a result of mental disease or defect, he lacks the substantial capacity to appreciate the wrongfulness of his action, or to conform his conduct to the requirements of law." The interviewer's blank look told him he was using language too arcane for the man on the street. He added, "Mental illness may undermine the essential ability to tell whether what one is doing is wrong. It may also hamper the ability to control one's actions."

Control had become a key word in the Outray case. Whatever self-restraint Randy himself had failed to exercise in the woods on that October morning, his defense team had kept him tightly under wraps ever since. He made no public statement, nor did he venture off the grounds of the family estate. The media was free to make what it would of both his past and his future.

*

I confronted my own past and future one afternoon in early December. It was my birthday, a day of crisp breeze and rare watery sunlight. I celebrated with a late day pilgrimage to St. John's Cemetery, where my parents lay together under a single lump of granite. Beside them, under separate polished markers, lay Brian and Rory. The red maple we had planted for my father was growing to shelter them all. Scattered crocus and lilies of the valley waited to bloom over them in the spring.

I had brought no flowers but I knelt briefly at each grave, letting the tears come as they always did and running gentle fingers over the names carved on my parents' headstone. Daniel Ryan, whose death had come with swift implacability. Margaret Campbell Ryan, whose life had slipped away by inches, numbering her among the dead long before her body gave up the struggle. She had dreaded the thought of becoming a burden, but Alzheimer's had steadily turned her into one. I had stood by her, as I later stood by my sister, torn by pity and grief, and by loathing of what their plight had done to me. There had been no escape from it then, only endurance. I still endured.

As I rose and stepped back from the headstone, I had the curious impression of somehow standing back from my life as well. In doing my duty to my family, I had become a stranger to myself, not only bereaved but miserably outcast, drifting with no clear aim, resenting the life I had been thrust into. I had behaved like a spoiled child who, because she cannot have the whole cake, refuses to eat at all. I had been waiting for life to offer itself back to me on its old terms. I finally understood that it wasn't going to.

Beyond the darkening paths of the cemetery, a yellow blur of streetlights suddenly stippled the gray sky, illumining the tiny specks of snow that had begun to fall. They were hardly big enough to be called flakes, certainly they were not the fat, lacy shapes of my childhood but, like a child, I raised my face and stuck out my tongue to taste their cold sweetness.

CHAPTER THIRTEEN

The river made all the sound there was. The air was still, the tangled boughs of leafless trees quiet under the falling snow. To my right, the sliding sparkle of water murmured beside the delicate shells of ice just beginning to skim its edges. A little way off the path stood a small gazebo that, in the sunlight of high summer, offered cooling shade and a charming view of the river. On a chilly December evening, it tendered refuge only to ghosts.

An owl swept past like the shadow of a flying cloud and startled me into turning. As I did, a second shadowy figure detached itself from the gloom not a hundred feet from where I stood. There was something familiar in the set of the shoulders and the easy, springing gait, and when he passed under the streetlamp at the side entrance to the cemetery, I recognized the bearded face of David Maitland. It had been ten days since the mock jury meeting and our lunch together at the Sandwich Board. I thought he glanced my way as he hesitated by the gate and I made to call out a greeting, then, remembering his abrupt departure from Kerrin's office that day, decided against it and turned away. One did not visit a cemetery hoping to find company. If the well-tended graves of St. John's could not grant solace, they did offer solitude and a reassuring measure of indifference.

I went on slowly toward the same exit that David Maitland had used. Here and there, the dark outlines of formal plantings were visible, groups of bushes and small ornamental trees dividing the sentinel rows of tombstones that flowed inland from the riverbank. A sundial stood knee-deep in a riot of low-growing rose bushes. I paused beside it, imagining the thick, sweet smell that would bloom along with the frilled little flowers.

Just inside the gate was a double grave still too fresh to bear the weight of a headstone. A temporary marker read "Forrester" and a sheaf of lilies blanketed the mound not yet settled back to earth. I remembered that the same flowers had graced the leafy copse where Susan and Tracy Forrester had died and I wondered if David Maitland's hand had laid those as well, and if so, why.

The snow was falling more heavily now. I was glad I'd worn duck boots and a duffel coat. I snugged the collar of my jacket up around my neck and pulled the wrought iron gate shut behind me.

My own street jogged south from Main. I stopped at the corner, beguiled by the smell of roasting chestnuts. During the summer months, Yuri Ivanov sold ice creams from a stand but tonight he was shaking a pan of rich, dark nuts over an open gas jet that hissed and flamed with the stirring breeze. Traffic slid past with the soft hush of wet tires, headlights glowing like ripe lemons through the falling snow. From the wine bar across the street came the sound of piano music overlaid by the animated chatter of young executives enjoying a social half hour before heading home. The window glittered like Aladdin's cave with row on row of bottled ruby and amber and purple.

I dug in my pockets for some loose change, grinning at Yuri in triumph as I came up with a dollar's worth to place in his outstretched hand. He might have been anywhere from twenty to forty years old. He had the bulk of a middle-aged man but his head seemed a little too large for his body and his face was as bland and unlined as a child's. As he accepted my coins, Yuri ducked his head with a shy smile and proffered a bag of steaming chestnuts as though they were a gift from the Magi. Greedily, I bit into one, drawing breath at the heat with a whoop that made him laugh out loud.

At her newsstand next to him, Yuri's mother glanced up sharply from the evening editions of the *Barker* and the *Express Press*. Fingerless black gloves could not disguise the elegance of Irina's tapering hands any more than the tightly wound scarf hid the delicate contours of her face. Though she had been born many years after the last tsar might have received her, her grace evoked images of an Imperial court far removed from this street corner. Her air of refinement made the gossipy tabloids in her hand seem even more tawdry.

I winced at the headlines.

Little Tracy Forrester could only be a sympathetic character, but snide journalistic pens denounced her mother in an exclusive to the *Barker* called "If you knew Susie (like I knew Susie) . . ."

I have noticed it before, this tendency when something bad happens to someone, to believe she must have done something to deserve it. Maybe disapprobation of the victim assuages our fear of becoming victims ourselves: if we can identify the fatal flaw that makes one woman the object of rape and murder, maybe we can modify our own behavior to avoid a similar end.

According to the papers, Susan Forrester had had a penchant for exhibitionism that put Madonna in the shade.

"Where do they get this garbage?" I said.

Irina answered gravely. "Like secret police—they use informed sources. They pay bartenders and hotel doormen. The journalists here make little jokes about it. They say Woodward and Bernstein had Deep Throat, tabloids have Deep Pockets."

"Do you suppose any of it is true?" I asked.

Irina shrugged. "Truth is not selling newspapers."

I thought about that as I munched on a chestnut, breathing its fragrance and holding the warmth of the bag close as I walked the final blocks home.

The message light on my phone was blinking when I got there.

"Hi. This is Brent William? I don't know if you remember me, but, like, I met you at Kerrin Adams's office for that mock jury thing? Anyway, I didn't know who you were then, but, when I phoned Metcalf College—I was trying to find someone who could help me with this idea I have?—they gave me your name. So, what I was wondering, is, like . . ."

The machine cut him off. A minute later the breathless voice resumed.

"Hi. This is Brent William again? I think your machine just cut me off. If I leave you my number, could you, maybe, give me a call back? I'd really appreciate it."

Since he had gotten my number from Metcalf College, I was pretty sure Brent was calling about "Alternatives." Some students want a more detailed outline of the course than the syllabus provides and I was happy to give it. Dealing with their concerns before things start was much easier than coping with their frustrations later. The fall term at Metcalf was just winding down. I was committed to teaching the winter session, but I wasn't sure I wanted to continue after that. I was getting restless.

As I made a note of Brent's number, the phone trilled in my hand and startled me into dropping the receiver. It bounced off the side of the table with a crash that must have hurt the ear at the other end of the line.

"Sorry about that," I said, snatching at the receiver before it could bounce again.

"Well, that's one way of discouraging unwanted callers."

I stammered something inane, surprised at hearing the voice and at my easy recognition of it. Even over the phone, the faint undertone of humor was unmistakable. It brought the image of hot peppers, rather than lilies, to mind. As if he could read my thought, David Maitland said, "I hope you don't mind my calling. I thought I saw you at the cemetery this afternoon, but I was afraid of intruding. I, uh, feel I should apologize for rushing off the other day. I enjoyed our lunch, and I rather wondered if you'd care to have dinner with me on Friday? I promise to feed you something milder than the burger at The Sandwich Board."

I hesitated. It had been years since I had last been on a date, not counting the odd foray to the theater with a cousin or an old family friend. By and large, the men I knew were either too married or too newly divorced to hold any attraction for me. I didn't know exactly what David Maitland's status was but I hadn't seen a wedding ring or the telltale signs of one recently removed when we had lunch. Now, remembering his puckish grin and the lovely bone structure of his hands, I decided to take a chance, and I was surprised by a springtime lift to my spirits when he said, "Great. Friday then. Pick you up at seven." I was still smiling when the doorbell rang ten minutes later. I hadn't felt so popular in years.

Kerrin stood on the step, laden with an assortment of bags and bottles, looking like a packhorse with an inflated rubber bridle. Her hands were too full of groceries to accommodate the strings of a dozen balloons, which she held clenched between her teeth.

I had not spoken to my sister since that day of revelation in her office. The balloons were a peace offering.

"Happy Birthday, Nini," Kerrin said, and I reached to pull the strings gently from her mouth.

"They're helium," she added, daring me to loose the kaleidoscopic mass into the room. I let them go, one by one. They floated on eddies from the still-open door, around the newel post and up toward the ceiling. They clustered like butterflies in the alcove by the fireplace.

While Kerrin uncorked a bottle of champagne, "From Oenophile, of course; Gerard recommended it," I lifted plates from the cupboard and unwrapped fragrant take-out bundles from Ristorante Tarina: tiny ravioli stuffed with meat, long tubes of pasta curled around exotic cheeses and drowned in a delicately flavored sauce, a creamy froth of meringue. I looked from the feast on the counter to my sister's smiling face.

"It's exactly the menu we had at your twenty-first *and* your twenty-fifth. We kind of skipped over thirty, so . . . Gino prepared it all himself."

I set a match to the fire while she poured the wine. She lifted her glass to me. Firelight spun and spangled up through a million bubbles. Balancing plates on our knees, we ate and laughed and talked like castaways unexpectedly rescued from their desert island, unable to get their fill of food or companionship.

"Remember when Mom brought that can of peas over for Thanksgiving?"

"And thought it was a bottle of wine, and told Brian to decant it?"

"Remember the day she almost set the house on fire, when she put the groceries into the oven, bag and all?"

At the time, there had been nothing even remotely funny about the events that signaled disintegration. Now, amid the commonplace of laughter, even the most painful memory was one to cherish.

A log in the fireplace fell apart, sending a shower of sparks flying upward. I rose and poked it back into place, savoring the contentment of the moment. I should have known that life is too complex for such facile endings.

CHAPTER FOURTEEN

The fire had dwindled, the champagne bottle was empty, and the debris of our impromptu party littered the room. I started collecting plates and forks.

Over the muted clatter, Kerrin said, "Leave that alone for a minute. There's something I need to show you."

I subsided into my chair. Kerrin pulled her soft leather bag up from beside the couch and rummaged in it briefly before extracting what looked like a CD. She held it in her hand as if weighing it.

"I'd better give you some background first." Gone was the bantering tone, back was the studied professionalism, and I marveled at the speed with which my sister had switched personas with the trial consultant. It was like moving from one room to another, flipping off the light in one, switching it on in the other.

Kerrin said, "From time to time, amid more run-of-the-mill theft and drug cases, I represent people accused of pretty terrible crimes, and sometimes, not often, but sometimes, I get a few nasty letters in the mail as a result. That's okay," she waved aside my protest. "That's okay. I can deal with that. But this time, with the Outray case, I've gotten something different, and I'm not sure what to do with it."

My eye went to the disk Kerrin was holding out to me. I took it from her gingerly, not sure I wanted its dreadful secret exposed, then slipped it into the player and pressed a few buttons.

There were no opening credits. It was not a professional film but a home video collage of a handsome man and a beautiful young woman holding a baby; helping a toddler learn to walk; blowing out the candles on a birthday cake. There was nothing remarkable about the little group or what they were doing. This was simply the record of a loving couple watching their daughter grow up. There was nothing to suggest that the wife and the daughter would one day soon be butchered in the woods not far from their home.

"This came with it." Kerrin handed me a folded sheet of paper.

"You bitch" it said. *"How can you defend that murdering bastard. Nothing can excuse what he did, or what you are doing to my family now. Look at them! Just look at them. And remember who the real victims are."*

On the screen, Tracy Forrester was hugging a ginger kitten and giggling at the caress of a rough pink tongue. I had a sudden image of a small boy perched high on the shoulder of a handsome man, laughing and clutching a stuffed bear named Ted. The child's image faltered and the screen went blank.

Pain has its uses. It gives you time to think about what life does to other people.

I said shakily, "That poor man. What are you going to do?"

I expected a routine, automatic response of kindness but it didn't come.

"I thought of calling the police."

"The police! Why on earth?"

"This is harassment. Mel Deloitte hasn't received anything like it and he's the boy's lawyer. Obviously, Ian Forrester's centering me out because I'm a woman and he thinks I'm an easier target for the sympathy vote. The problem is, if I make this public, the sympathy will all be on his side and that won't make defending Randy Outray any easier. What's the matter with you?" she said. "You're looking at me like I'm speaking in tongues."

"I don't believe what I'm hearing. The man who sent you this is in pain. His wife and his child have been murdered. The press is doing a song and dance about how Randy Outray may be guilty but not responsible, and they're trashing the reputation of the dead woman. This is a cry for justice. Ian Forrester is asking you to keep some perspective on this case, to remember that his family, not Randy Outray, are the victims. And you're talking about calling the police! As far as I'm concerned, you should be writing a note of apology."

"Come off it. My job is to find the best defense I can for the guy accused of the crime, not to send flowers to the people trying to put him away. I can't afford to look at anybody other than my client as the victim."

"But Kerrin, he's practically admitted that he did it! You saw the reaction of the mock jury. You can't tell me that anything you say in court, even if Randy Outray is a total head case, is going to buy him innocence."

"No. But what we say, and the way we say it, can buy him pity and that, Mel can trade in for acquittal."

CHAPTER FIFTEEN

As soon as the door opened, I was struck by the barrenness of the apartment. Brent William's living room didn't even have a rug on the floor. There was a ratty sofa, a 30-inch TV and a leafy green plant with the gift card still attached. In one corner, housed on its packing box, was an elaborate computer setup with a padded half chair so odd-looking, it had to be a masterpiece of ergonomic design. I could imagine Brent's gangly frame balanced on it while his mind was lost inside the machine in front of him.

At the moment, his long legs straddled the arm of the sofa as he outlined his plans for a venture called "Roadblocks." I had accepted his offer of coffee while I heard him out. The longer I listened, the more firmly convinced I became that an assistance bureau for fledgling entrepreneurs and inventors would be worthwhile. Brent needed more specific help than "Alternatives" could provide.

There was none of the breathless hesitation I had heard in his voice on the phone. Nor any of the rising inflection.

"People waste a lot of valuable time," he said, "Aimlessly surfing the net instead of zeroing in on the information that's really pertinent. Some of them get completely lost."

"Hence 'Roadblocks'?"

"That's right. Have a look at the logo I designed. What do you think?"

Black lettering stood out boldly against an orange background that reminded me of road construction signs. Brent had printed "ROADBLOCKS," enclosed the word in a circle and drawn a line through it.

"Clients will hire me to teach their staff how to use the Internet efficiently. You know, you can do everything online now. But if you don't know how to separate the wheat from the chaff, especially if you're researching, you waste a lot of time and money."

I nodded. "And of course the advertisers don't help. They track which sites you visit and throw out banners aimed at distracting you."

The Internet pushed life beyond the old physical barriers of time and space; it allowed us to roam the world without ever leaving home. But it fostered a kind of nonlinear literacy. Patience was becoming obsolete. People were increasingly unwilling to read anything of substantive length requiring concentration. They wanted brevity, fast-moving images, instant stimulation, constant gratification. We have created a world in which the worst sin is to be boring.

I suggested as much to Brent. He shook his head emphatically. "We've created whole new forums for discussion and for transmitting information. People read more, research more, question more than they ever did before. I have a niece who's three. I figure by the time she gets to university—if there is such a thing then—she'll be able to access all the world's information via her wristwatch. I don't see anything wrong with that. Wasn't it Einstein who said, 'never memorize anything you can look up?'"

I sipped my coffee. "Are you planning to expand this service beyond Kingsport?"

Brent laughed. "Of course. It's Internet-based, I'll sell it on the Internet. Which means around the globe."

His earnest intelligence had me hooked. I knew he was right. Real power now rests with those capable of absorbing, manipulating, and marketing information. Brent had the technical know-how; I had the business acumen. And "Roadblocks," or something like it, could provide an essential element for my IdeasCenter. With a shock of surprise, I realized that the Center was moving steadily from fantasy to reality. My file of questions and answers, how-to's and what-not-to's was fast becoming a blueprint for a viable business. It was an exhilarating thought.

"Did you ever read Ray Bradbury?" I said. *"Fahrenheit 451?"*
Brent nodded.

"Remember the fire captain? His idea was to cram people full of noncombustible data. He said, 'Chock them so damned full of facts they feel stuffed, but absolutely brilliant with information.' He wrote that in the fifties. Now TV and computers have made it real. People are overwhelmed by the sheer volume of information available to them." I grinned. "You'd better help them sort it out."

It was after seven when I shrugged back into my coat. Brent offered me a sandwich. I said no thanks. Sonja Reid had taken up most of my afternoon with eleventh hour fussing for The Party. The caterer had prepared samples of the finger foods he had to offer and Sonja needed to make her final choices. We had spent the afternoon taste-testing. It was not arduous work. We approved scallop shells filled with some delicious concoction of creamed crab; crisp pastries bulging with mushroom and chicken and lobster; petit fours bland with almonds; small, frosted glasses of whipped cream tangy with strawberries and wine.

Afterward, I made a close inspection of the house. The last two weeks had seen a flurry of activity from the cleaning staff as, corner by corner, under my critical eye, Reidmore was readied for the event of the year. Chandeliers were washed luster by luster, mirrors were polished, parquet floors waxed, furniture and rugs spirited from one room to another. Outside, floodlights had been fitted up and a fountain like a firework stood ready to shoot its sparkling trails to a December sky. On the day before the party, a small army was scheduled to deliver flowers that would denude greenhouses for miles around.

For a woman accustomed to such star-studded occasions, Sonja seemed unaccountably nervous about this one. Mentally reviewing the preparations for the hundredth time, I could find nothing to justify her brittle air and finally concluded that the cause must lie with the guest list. Sonja had drawn up the list herself, addressing the envelopes in her own distinctive hand, so, although I knew the number of invitees and could easily predict who most of them must be, I guessed there must be a wild card or two giving her pause.

As usual at mid-month, I balanced Sonja's ledger and paid her outstanding accounts. At this time of year, there were many. I made out checks to the dressmaker, the wine importer, and the electrician. Clipped to the bill from the printer who had supplied the invitations for the party was a copy of the guest list. Curiosity struggled briefly with good manners and easily won.

Next to each name on the list was a tick mark indicating the invitation had been sent. A second column, for replies, showed only the rare "x" where someone had declined. These were people who regularly spent the Christmas season elsewhere. My eye stopped with a little shock at the tick beside the name Outray.

There was no reason, I supposed, why the Outrays should not be invited this year as they were every year, though I was surprised to see that they had accepted. If my son stood accused of murder, I am not sure I would have the nerve to face my neighbors. It would be interesting to see just how far aplomb could carry them, though it was discomfiting to know I would soon be meeting them face to face. I wondered how closely reality would match the media image. My interest had been further piqued at Mel Deloitte's.

Deloitte's study easily qualified for earthquake relief, the usual clutter supplanted by an Olympian mass of briefing notes, research texts, and scrap paper that had not yet made it as far as the shredder. I knew better than to touch any of it. The piles only looked haphazard. In fact, they were carefully arranged to give the lawyer easy access to whatever facts or ideas he wanted to reference, but I couldn't help noticing that many of them dealt with the subject of abuse. He had been researching the topic heavily, no doubt seeking a new avenue of escape for his client. The mock jury had been unwilling to accept a straight plea of insanity. Would they be more open to an abuse excuse? I would find out soon enough. Kerrin had recalled us to duty.

CHAPTER SIXTEEN

I hardly recognized Kerrin's secretary, Louise. The stiff golden locks had given way to black with generous swatches of gray, the tight curls shorn to within an inch of her scalp. The overall effect was not unlike a poodle whose coat has been mangled by an inexpert groomer. Oddly enough, on Louise it didn't look bad.

Around the conference table, seven mock jurors greeted each other with polite handshakes. David held on to mine longer than good manners strictly dictated. I didn't object. Brent waved from his end of the table. No one mentioned the absence of Daintry Gregg.

While we took our seats, Louise passed around a tray of pastries.

Kerrin got straight to work. She looked drawn, the fine skin under her eyes smudged with fatigue. She took no special notice of me.

"Let's talk about TV," she said. "TV in the courtroom. JusticeTV. I'm sure we've all watched it at some point in the last few years."

Heads nodded. "It's like a good soap," Lila said. She looked as trashy as ever, waving blood-red nails as though drying a new coat of polish. "There's always some new drama going on."

Jerry snorted. "Soap, my ass. This is living history. We're witnessing our judicial system in action here."

"Do you really think so?" someone said. And someone else said, "Absolutely not. The presence of TV cameras completely changes the dynamics of a courtroom."

Opinions blew around the table.

"I've seen prosecutors who are as dull as ditchwater. They make a terrible impression on film."

"Yeah, well I've heard of some who spend all their time preparing a case in front of a mirror, trying to come up with some dramatic gestures to use to make themselves look better."

"What difference does it make what they look like on film? It's the evidence they present that matters."

"You think so? You think juries aren't swayed by appearance? Or by public opinion?"

"Yeah, but what drives that opinion? I'll tell you what. The media. They take seven hours of testimony and reduce it to five minutes. Makes the whole thing incomprehensible and biased as hell."

"Bull. TV shows you stuff as it's actually happening. How can that be biased?"

"If you knew you were going to be on national television, wouldn't you make sure your shirt was pressed and your hair was combed? These people play to the camera like crazy. It's a kick for them being recognized on the street like a celebrity."

Kerrin spoke above the growing din. "You're saying, all of you, in one way or another, that the TV image has a major impact on how we view the world. Whether you think it's a distorted view or not, television influences our actions, our reactions . . ."

"Yeah."

"Absolutely."

"What about regular programming? The sitcoms, the adventure series . . . what kind of impact do they have?"

Thomas Lyons said, "We have to be careful of course, how much influence we allow them to have. They're just entertainments, after all. Take them with a grain of salt and so on."

"Take them with a grain of salt," Kerrin said. "Okay. But do you think everyone does that, or can do that? Do you think some people are more capable than others of drawing a line between what is true and what is not, what is honest reporting and what has been magnified for effect, what has been done as entertainment and what represents the real world?"

No one answered. From Jerry's mulish assertion that the camera never lies, to Lila's delight in real life drama to Thomas Lyons's pompous cynicism, it was clear that no two of them were affected by the media in exactly the same way. It was the response Kerrin was looking for.

"We can never know exactly how another person perceives and interprets what he sees on television. What we do know is that the electronic screen has an amazing power to mesmerize. D'you realize that young Americans today spend about as much time in front of a television as they do in a classroom? That's right. At midnight, every night, nearly 2 million children under the age of twelve are still watching TV. The average adult watches more than thirty hours a week. Almost as much time as they spend working. And we know what the content of many shows is: violence. Kids see more acts of violence in half an hour of television than most would encounter in a dozen lifetimes. They become inured to it, they begin to accept it as the norm. They begin to have trouble telling the difference between the images they see on the screen and reality." Around the table, heads were beginning to nod agreement. "Behaviorists are noticing that kids who watch a lot of TV are acting out in the playground, with their schoolmates, on the street. They call it television violence intoxication. TVI."

Heads nodded. Jerry muttered, "Here we go with the intoxication theory again."

Kerrin pressed her point. "TVI was first used as a defense argument in a case in Florida about twenty years ago. The courts are beginning to accept that repeated exposure to violent programs on television can lead an individual to commit violent acts."

Reaction was more subtle now: a raised eyebrow, a thoughtful expression. I had a vivid recollection of the WKPT broadcast filmed in Randy Outray's home. I remembered how a television screen had dominated the room and I speculated on the role the media might play in a family so often a target of it. From the expressions on their faces, so did the many of my fellow jurors. Only David still looked wary.

"This ranks right up there with the Twinkie Defense, doesn't it?" he said. "For those of you who don't know," he explained, "That particular argument claimed that the accused ate too much junk food and the resulting chemical imbalance in his system was to blame for his behavior. It's the current vogue in defending someone in court these days; blame their criminal acts on some other force in their lives. Call it a syndrome. Make the abuser seem like the abused."

"Some of those syndromes are real," objected Lila. "What about the Super Bowl Sunday one? It's a proven fact that more women get beat up that day than any other."

"Actually . . ." Thomas Lyons began.

Jerry cut him off. "Hey, she's right. There is such a thing as a syndrome. I mean, d'you remember the Menendez Brothers? I saw that on TV."

"They weren't acquitted."

"Maybe not, but they got a mistrial. Because some experts testified about parental abuse."

"Everyone knows that years of emotional or sexual abuse by a parent can cause a person to lose control," said Lila. Her tone was authoritative, her expertise gleaned from years of soap opera viewing.

"How did we get from TV violence to parental abuse?" I asked. "Is anyone seriously suggesting that Randy Outray's parents abused him? Or that he killed two people because he watched too much TV?"

There was some confusion around the table as people tried to sort out their opinions. Kerrin shot me a look. I saw where she was going. A specific charge of abuse might not even be necessary. It could be enough to create the illusion, to have an expert or two suggest it. These days, we accepted excuses for the most vile behaviors. Instead of individual responsibility, we have societal blame. The violent act can come first; an excuse for it can be found later. Kerrin had been right when she said that the defense didn't have to prove anything. It only had to create doubt.

"Reasonable doubt," I'd amended.

Kerrin had smiled. "Of course."

CHAPTER SEVENTEEN

David picked me up at seven on the dot and ushered me to the car. I sat rather shyly beside him, my hands in my lap, watching the road twist up to meet us as we picked our way down the icy hill to the bridge before gathering speed on River Road. Frost-covered trees streamed by, drenched briefly in the gold of our headlights, dimming, fleeing, gone. The city glittered with Christmas lights whose reflections swayed and bobbed in the dark waters of the Old Harbor.

We had a wonderful dinner at a place where clothes didn't matter and the food was excellent. We didn't dance there, because, we agreed, eating was too important for the distraction of gymnastics but later, somewhere else, we danced and later still, we went to a club and listened to jazz and drank brandy and laughed a lot and then, at last, drove home.

David was an easy person to be with, direct, undemanding, not interpreting occasional silences as personal insults nor rushing to fill the space.

He asked about my job and my family and I found myself talking quite naturally about Brian and Rory and my life on the fringes of Kingsport's rich and famous. In turn, he talked of his own, much broader world as an engineer engaged to build bridges in remote areas of the globe. He didn't specify what business had brought him from Pago Pago to Kingsport, but I had the impression it was something personal, though not an ex-wife or old flame.

"I have a theory about marriage," he said. "How many people do you know who rushed into marriage at twenty-one or twenty-two, only to have the whole thing fall apart once they grew up and the passion died? I believe that if you can withstand the early impulse to jump into marriage, you're safe till you hit your thirties.

By then, passion is still a factor but it's likely to be grounded in something more substantial than simple lust. You've had time to look around, try a few things, decide what you want from a partner. And what you're willing to give."

"Lots of early marriages succeed," I objected. "And plenty of later ones fail. How do they fit your theory?"

He grinned. "They don't. So I ignore them. I only consider the evidence that supports my own hypothesis."

"That's not very scientific."

"Maybe not. But it gives me an excuse for still being single."

"Do you need an excuse?"

A waiter sidled up and deposited our bill, laying it between us with a bright meaningless smile. Not like the good old days, when they knew for a fact that the gentleman was paying.

We collected our coats, buttoning them tight in anticipation of the cold blast that met us when we stepped outside. David turned the defroster on high. It took a few minutes to clear the windshield.

"How did you wind up at Kerrin's?" I asked.

"I met her through the friend of a friend. The mock jury thing sounded interesting and I was at a bit of a loose end, so I more or less invited myself to join. How did you?"

"I'm a regular. Kerrin is my sister."

He gave me a swift sidelong glance and the car swerved as it hit a patch of ice. David regained the wheel easily, but the light mood of the evening seemed to drop from him. He drove on in an abstracted, frowning silence that I put down to the slippery conditions and the winding road.

It was one-thirty when we reached my place. I invited him in for a nightcap but he pleaded an early engagement. "Rain check?" he said, as he waited for me to unlock the door.

"Sure," I said, and held out my hand.

He took it and leaned down and kissed my cheek. His beard tickled. We looked at each other, my hand still in his. David bent his head and kissed me again, this time on my lips.

I watched him down the drive and he dipped his headlights twice, briefly, in farewell. I shut the door and leaned hard against it, wishing he had stayed.

*

The next day passed in a whirl. I spent the morning at Reidmore, supervising the arrangement of flowers brought in by the vanload. Tiers of pink and red poinsettias were stacked to resemble Christmas trees, with fairy lights twinkling among their leaves. Pine wreaths were interlaced with tiny rosebuds; holly swathed the main staircase; and vase after vase was filled with sprays of white anemone. The musicians tuned their instruments in the upper gallery; the caterer's assistants laid out silverware; the bartenders set bottles of champagne on ice. At one, Sonja returned from Anitra's Beauty Salon. Every visible inch of her had been styled and buffed to a high gloss. In the noon light, she looked slightly surreal but in the muted glow of candles and dimmed chandeliers, she would look magnificent. She laid one perfectly manicured hand on my arm.

"My dear, you should have told me you had a friend. I never thought . . . but of course, I would have been more than happy to invite him. Anyway, Max has taken care of it and I'm so looking forward to meeting him."

"Him who?"

"David Maitland, of course."

"David?" I repeated stupidly.

"Yes. Max had a game of squash with him at the Clubbe. Absolutely charming, he says. Some kind of engineer. Anyway, this David mentioned that he was a friend of yours, and naturally, Max invited him along tonight. Isn't that nice?" She patted my arm. "But you will still keep an eye on things for me, won't you."

*

Dressing for my first dance in years . . . and David somewhere among the crowd of guests. I fought to keep the butterflies at bay but my fingers shook as I opened a bar of scented soap and bobby pins scattered like confetti when I gathered my hair high onto my head. The blue velvet gown soothed my nerves a little and my mother's diamond eardrops very nearly calmed me.

By nine-thirty, the Reidmore Ball was well under way. Max and Sonja had finished receiving and their place near the banked flowers at the foot of the staircase was empty.

The hall was brilliant with a shifting mass of people, the men elegant in black tie, the women dazzling in shimmery gowns and radiant smiles. Mel Deloitte was there, partnering a blonde with slanting eyes and a beautiful mouth. She was dancing very close to him, talking rapidly, with flickering upward glances through long lashes. He was smiling.

On the far side of the room, Sonja was charming an elderly man whose face looked vaguely familiar but whose name I couldn't place. Max sat on a small sofa chatting with General Sanderson. The general had stationed his wheelchair by the fireplace, out of the way of the dancers, but well in the line of sight of anyone headed for the bar. His wife, looking wonderful in a gown of royal purple, was being lectured by a woman with dyed hair, wearing emeralds and dramatic black.

The music stopped and people drifted to the sides of the room. In the moment of silence that followed, John and Zoe Outray appeared in the doorway as though cued by a stage director. They were flanked by their children, Randy and Simone.

Every eye turned to look at them, and for the space of a heartbeat, there was total silence in the room. Then, somewhere to my left, a glass shattered; a woman gave a shrill little laugh; and in the gallery upstairs, the musicians began to play again. Max and Sonja were on their feet, he with hand outstretched in polite welcome, she with the gracious smile of a hostess firmly in place.

Murmured comments rippled around the room.

The man next to me said, "Hell of a nerve."

His companion sniffed. "Pathetic really, isn't it? And just look at that dress!"

The dress in question was worn by Simone Outray, the least advertised member of the clan. Drab silver drapery hung in folds on a frame too gawky and unformed to carry such sophisticated styling. I knew the girl must be at least sixteen, but she had the thin shapelessness of a twelve-year old and the sullen look of a bad-tempered child.

The woman beside her, on the other hand, looked the part the way her daughter never would. Perfectly groomed, she radiated chilly elegance. Her husband's austere profile was somewhat marred by the bulbous red nose of the heavy social drinker.

Of course it was their son, John Randall Outray III, who claimed most of the attention.

Having seen his face so often in the news, it was intriguing to see him in the flesh. He was taller than his father, with the lean, hard musculature of an athlete. He favored the unkempt, who-gives-a-damn look of stubbled jaw and messy hair but his gray silk suit was from Armani. He looked surprisingly young, completely self-possessed, and curiously blank around the eyes.

There was no time for a more detailed appraisal of the family. Party guests swarmed around them like baseball fans around their heroes. Several women, not all of them young, reached out to touch Randy. I half-expected him to pull out a handkerchief, wipe his brow with it and throw it to the adoring crowd. Notoriety breeds its own cult worship, and here, among the members of the Clubbe and the Porsche set, a murder trial had simply become the latest party game. I doubted that Randy would fare so well in the streets, where placard-waving protestors insisted on "Death for the Angel," and new petitions were signed daily demanding safer streets for women and children.

Sonja caught my eye and used hers to indicate the kitchen.

It was easy to slip unnoticed through the crowd to check on the supplies of food and liquor, much more difficult not to look too obviously for David. I wondered what his impression would be of the criminal in our midst.

When his voice said, "Hello there" just behind me, I jumped like a thief caught in the act of stealing the silver.

"You startled me," I said a shade breathlessly, as David, looking incredibly handsome in a dinner jacket, appeared at my elbow.

"Where have you been hiding?"

The music swelled into a waltz, obliterating my reply. David spun me onto the floor.

His voice murmured in my ear, "Surprised?"

"Not entirely. Sonja told me you were invited."

He raised an eyebrow. "Do you mind?"

"Be my guest."

He smiled and swept me round with the music in a quick turn. A pillar swirled past, a group of men, a wheelchair. In the middle of the bright kaleidoscope loomed a gray shadow. Randy Outray was watching the dancers, like a spider at the knot of a web. I shook my head to dispel the fancy. David slanted a look at me and I gave him a brilliant smile. We were dancing at the edge of the room, near French windows that stood open to the mild night. Before I knew quite what he intended, we were out of the room and on the wide veranda, slipping out of the crowd as easily as a floating twig slides into a backwater. The music followed us through the long windows. We danced without speaking along the moonlit arcade and in again through the windows of the library, where firelight warmed the deserted shadows. In one of the logs, I could hear the whine and bubble of resin. The music sounded very far away. Still without speaking, David stopped. His arms tightened around me and I melted into them.

*

When at length he let me go and spoke, his voice was unsteady. But it still held that little undertone of laughter that was unmistakably his.

Holding me at arm's length, he said, "Well, aren't you going to ask it?"

"Ask what?"

"What any other woman would have asked right away. Why I crashed the party."

I said, "It's enough that you're here."

David stared at me for a moment. He said something in a queer, tight voice, then pulled me to him again. He didn't kiss me, but held me tightly and spoke over my head into the darkness.

"Nina . . . Nina, listen."

"I'm listening."

A shadow stabbed across the carpet, cutting the light in two. Someone had come to the doorway and stopped dead in the path of the glow from the hall. I jumped and swung around.

Someone drawled, "Well, excuse me."

Whoever it was, was backed against the light, so I couldn't see his face, but I felt David stiffen and his hand tighten convulsively on my shoulder. Then the figure turned away, toward the music and the light, and I saw that it was Randy Outray.

The moment passed. I let out a shaky breath. "Well," I said, as lightly as I could, "I'd better be getting back. I'm supposed to keep an eye on the caterers. If I'm not there, Sonja will be speculating wildly on the whys and wherefores."

"I don't suppose she'll have any doubts at all about the whys and wherefores," David said, and laughed.

I flushed and said tartly, "It's all very well for you, carrying on regardless, but I'm only the hired help. I've got to face her tomorrow."

There was a low murmur in the hallway as several other guests glanced in on their way by. I recognized one as an inveterate eyebrow raiser.

"I'd better go," I said again.

David hesitated, then bent and kissed me, a brief, hard kiss. "I'll see you home later," he said, and let me go.

*

The dining room was dazzling with people and gay with chatter and popping corks. I made my way through the crowd, trying to locate Sonja without actually catching her eye. She wasn't there. On the far side of the room, Randy Outray lounged against the wall, looking bored. One of the waiters offered him a glass of champagne, the caterer's assistant hard on his heels with a platter of hors d'oeuvres. Randy flapped a hand as though she were a persistent, annoying fly. As he turned away from her, the hooded eyes met mine. I saw them widen in recognition and sardonic amusement, then, slowly, deliberately, Randy Outray moved his tongue across his lips in an unmistakable gesture that brought the blood rushing to my cheeks. I turned and pushed my way back through the glittering crush of bodies.

I crossed the hallway, gained the stairs, and mounted them hurriedly, seeking the time and space to gather the scattered rags of my self-possession. I was nearly at the top when the catch of my sandal came loose and the sandal came off. As I stooped to pick it up, Simone Outray slipped out of one of the bedrooms. The lank hair had fallen forward to mask her face. She hurried by me on the stairs without a glance.

The sandal was my alibi. I waited politely for Simone to pass before I proceeded along the hall for the needed repairs. On the landing, a clock whirred to strike midnight. A thought touched me and I stopped short.

Midnight. A dropped slipper. And Prince Charming?

Maybe.

CHAPTER EIGHTEEN

The corridor led to a bedroom with an en suite guests could use. Quietly, I opened the door and went in.

Zoe Outray was sitting in an armchair by a curtained window. Her eyes were closed but she was not sleeping. I studied the famous face. She was, I supposed, about fifty years old, and still a lovely woman. Her skin was pale and clear and expertly made-up; her brows delicately drawn and arched with a faint arrogance. Her hair was sculptured silver. Only her mouth was too thin for beauty. In repose, she looked expensive, fragile, and about as approachable as the moon. Whatever her thoughts, they deepened the tiny wrinkles etching her eyes and mouth.

"Bring it here," she commanded in a cool, clear voice.

"Excuse me?" I said.

Zoe Outray roused herself briefly to look at me. She apologized with chilly grace for her mistake and murmured something about a headache. I hesitated. The remoteness of her manner made her difficult to read. Her features were perfectly composed; nothing ruffled the silvery surface. But I noticed that the fragile pink silk of the chair arm had ripped under her nails, and I felt an unexpected surge of pity.

"Mrs. Outray. Is there anything I can get for you?"

The gray eyes opened again but, before she could respond, the door opened and Simone came in carrying a steaming cup of what smelled like tea laced with brandy. She looked startled at the sight of me, bent to restrap my sandal. The cup she was carrying was overfull. As the girl bent to place it in her mother's hand, some of the tea slopped over the edge of the cup and onto the skirt of Zoe Outray's dress.

The effect, on both mother and daughter, was remarkable.

Simone's face, always pale, was now ash white. She stammered something that was meant to be an apology but her mother cut across it in a voice that bit like a whip.

"Look what you've done! You clumsy little bitch. Even getting a cup of tea is asking too much of you. Look at me! How can I go back downstairs with tea stains on my dress?"

"It's not that bad."

Simone spoke in a small shaken voice. Resentment had flattened her features into a sullen mask that made her look retarded. Something came and went in her mother's face. It was the merest flick of an expression, like the flash of a camera's shutter, but the girl took a quick step backward and I crossed the floor swiftly, taking the cup from her trembling hand and offering to fetch some soda from the kitchen to deal with the stains.

"Thank you, you're very good," Zoe Outray said. The words were pleasant, but formally spoken, and the smile had gone. She did not meet my eye. Sonja Reid may have placed me above the salt for the evening but her friend would be sure I kept to my own side of the table.

She had turned back to Simone and though the bite was gone, I heard the taunt in her voice as she said, "It's just as well that your forays into polite society are restricted to one or two a year. That crowd you hang around with obviously sets a very low standard."

I saw the swift upward slant of Simone's lashes. The sullen look deepened.

Something sparked inside me. Zoe Outray had every right to ignore my presence if she chose, but none at all to castigate her grown daughter in front of me, a stranger. I said as evenly as I could, "I know Sonja would expect me to take care of her guests. If Simone will come with me to the kitchen, I'll get her something for the stain."

I stopped. I had seen the faintest, least definable shade of what looked like amusement in Simone's face, but it was amusement at some joke I couldn't see. The impression was peculiarly unpleasant. In the next moment, it might have been illusion. Ducking her head, Simone scuttled to the door in my wake and I steered her toward the back stairs that led directly to the kitchen.

"Your mother must be under a terrible strain," I said.

"Are you a shrink or something?"

I ignored the rude tone.

Her anxiety, like her mother's anger, had seemed out of all proportion to the incident I had witnessed until I remembered some of my own mother's outbursts, when she learned that she had Alzheimer's. The hospital psychologist had explained that people coping with mortal illness, or great emotional stress, go through "steps" in their effort to reach some level of acceptance of their pain. One of the steps is anger. Anger needs a focus. And it is easier to zero in on something trivial that has gone awry than to try to encompass the enormity of the tragedy in your life. My mother's catharsis had come one morning when she discovered that a neighbor's dog had dug a small pit in the middle of her perennial garden. She had chased the animal away with a broom, shouting imprecations I never imagined she knew, before returning to weep over her ruined flowers as if they were lost souls.

I tried explaining something of this to Simone.

We stood at the end of the deserted upper hall. The girl listened with bad grace to my little homily, staring at the carpet, face set in the martyred lines of one accustomed to receiving lectures. Something dark and unreadable moved behind her still features. When I finished, her eyes came up to meet mine.

"You think my mother treats me like a moron because she's upset, is that it? You have no idea." She opened the door and started down the back stairs but she had only gone a few steps when she stopped and turned to face me again. "This isn't a new behavior for her, you know."

"Your brother . . ."

"My brother," Simone cut in, in a flat little voice, "Is a tin god who can do no wrong. Not in Mother's eyes." Resentment burned in every syllable and her voice hardened. "I know he's in big trouble—this is the worst so far—but I don't see why the whole family has to revolve around him. He's not the only one suffering because of it. God, I'd have to come down with some kind of terminal disease to be able to compete. Simone, the ugly duckling, should be hidden away in a closet. After all, she can't even carry a cup of tea without spilling it. But Randy, wonderful Randy, why he can get away with murder." She giggled as though she'd told a slightly naughty joke but the note of acid amusement in her voice made me as uncomfortable as the determined grievance she seemed bent on sharing with me.

"Simone . . . "

"She's always thought the sun rose and set on him. I was just an afterthought. A mistake. Randy is her golden boy. Don't you think there's something just a little bit sick about a fifty-year old woman fawning on her twenty-two-year old son?"

I was appalled at the venom my ill-advised attempt to help had unleashed. Desperately I reviewed my words, trying to understand how I had invited such dreadful confidences from this virtual stranger and trying to think of a way to dam the flow.

"And as for my Daddy, huh. He's too busy with other things to even notice. If he's not at the office, he's at the Clubbe, working out. I know what kind of 'working out' they do there. They think I don't, but I do. I'm not stupid."

She was in full cry now.

"Simone . . . " I said again, not wanting to hear.

"I wish they were dead," she said. "I wish they were all dead!"

Her voice cracked. She began to tremble.

We had reached the point where the staircase bent to create a small landing. Hurriedly I sat the girl down and, not knowing what else to do, put my arms around her, and rocked her as I had rocked my young nephew when he skinned his knee. Then, a kiss and a few soothing words had been all that was needed to set the world right. Now, holding this child-woman in my arms and understanding but little of her pain, it seemed to me that Rory had never seemed so completely gone. I said it to myself deliberately; so dead.

The thought stilled my rocking. The girl in my arms had stopped trembling; her eyes were dry and I wondered, fleetingly, if she ever shed tears, or if her pain went too deep for them. I stood up, smoothing the wrinkles out of my dress. Simone retreated once again behind the sulky mask, and insisted on taking the stain remover back up to her mother herself. I didn't argue. I had no wish to become mixed up any further in the Outrays' domestic tragedy.

*

The party wound down around two in the morning. I held David's hand as we walked to his car. Snow dusted the boughs of the pine trees lining the drive and sparkled in the moonlight. It reminded me of the angel hair my mother used to put on our Christmas tree.

"I always hated that stuff," David said. "It looked so pretty but every time I touched it, I got those sharp prickles in my hands."

I snuggled deeper into my coat. The evening had been a huge success. Sonja had thanked me for my help with a smile that promised a large bonus. She made no comment on my prolonged absence; she had seen me with Simone in the kitchen.

The remainder of the night had passed without incident. I watched Zoe Outray as she danced with her son. She looked radiant. Not a mark showed on her shimmering dress; the nasty little scene upstairs might never have taken place. As Randy smiled down at her, Simone's words echoed in my mind. What she had implied was nonsense, it had to be, born of the girl's unhappiness. And yet, I couldn't help wondering if there might not be something in it, if there wasn't something more than simple mother love to explain Zoe Outray's support, more, adoration of her son. Well, it was not my problem. Whatever I felt about the Outrays, however much I pitied the Forresters, their lives touched mine only peripherally. And if their lives were full of puzzles, it was no business of mine.

CHAPTER NINETEEN

David turned out to be a bit of a clown in bed, funny and inventive, generous and warm. It had been so long since I'd been with a man that I was nervous, afraid of disappointing him. He went slowly, giving me time. A touch. A kiss. An undemanding smoothing of his hand over my skin. I had forgotten how completely sensation can blot out thought. The little glow of smug self-satisfaction I felt afterward surprised me.

"What happened to that post-whatsit depression you're supposed to feel?"

"Hmm. That's only for amateurs."

"Oh, and you're a pro, is that it?"

"Remind me to resent that when I'm feeling more earthly."

It was almost dawn when we finally fell asleep.

I woke not long after, disturbed by a dream in which I stood balanced on the edge of a precipice. David's legs slanted diagonally across the bed, his right arm out-flung, constraining me to a sliver of mattress and a thin wedge of pillow. I found myself hoping the position wasn't habitual and smiled at the implications even as I drifted back to sleep.

"What do you like for breakfast?" I asked a few hours later.

He attempted a lewd grin, but it didn't mesh with the baggy eyes or the froggy voice. I laughed.

"If you're one of those insufferably cheery morning people, our relationship is doomed," he said.

We spent the day sprawled by the fire, reading the Sunday comics and rehashing The Party. Naturally, the Outrays and their coterie pulled focus.

"I can't believe that guy showing up, acting like some kind of pop star. He's practically admitted to murder, for God's sake!"

"He is out on bail," I pointed out. "There's no law against him going to a private party. I agree it's in poor taste . . . "

"Taste. That asshole butchered two people. Was that poor taste, too? Or just poor judgment? What about the poor victims?"

I stared, disconcerted by his sudden fury.

David was on his feet, pacing the room as he harangued me.

"The whole thing stinks. Did you hear them talking last night?" I stood on the fringes while Mel Deloitte held court there in the living room. He was talking as though getting Randy Outray acquitted was practically a done deal. "We just have to find the right buttons to push," he was saying. As though the truth had no part in it. As though making some excuse for what Outray did was enough to somehow right the balance. "You saw that mock jury — they were buying all that abuse crap. Enough of them on a real jury and Outray could walk! Hell, you were there. What do you think?"

He had been standing by the window, staring out at my garden. The snow was still falling, flattening the contours of my flower beds, and creating its own profile against the fence and the trees. David spun around to face me, stabbing a finger in my direction like a prosecutor with a hostile witness.

I answered quietly. "I think he might have a chance of getting off. Not through me, I don't believe in TV intoxication or junk food syndrome any more than you do. But you know as well as I do that finding excuses for violent behavior has become the fashion. The system allows for it. What is a jury, after all? It's twelve people of average intelligence applying their own values to the law. If a lawyer is lucky enough, or canny enough to pick the right ones . . . " I shrugged helplessly.

David argued, "But that doesn't make sense. If, as a society, we say an individual isn't responsible for his actions—for any reason—aren't we saying that he is, in fact, irresponsible? And doesn't that in itself make him a threat to the rest of us? If we absolve him of blame, shouldn't we also deny him trust, and keep him off the streets? Letting someone like that loose on society is like throwing a bomb into a crowd and waiting for it to explode."

I said, "You're saying good versus bad outweighs healthy versus sick."

"Damn right."

"But there's the sticking point. The concept of evil is hard to accept. There's no defense against evil. It's much more comfortable to find some excuse for abhorrent behavior, something that has gone wrong in a life. Then you can label it, and treat it, and maybe legislate against it."

"Treat it? You mean they can stick Randy Outray in a fancy private clinic somewhere and in a couple of years, maybe less, some expert will pronounce him cured. Then he'll be free. But Susan and Tracey Forrester will still be dead."

The bitterness in his voice was a warning. For a few minutes, neither of us spoke. Then David said, "The other night, you told me Kerrin Adams was your sister."

"That's right. She is. Why?"

"It's ironic, that's all."

"What is?"

"Susan Forrester was mine."

We were sitting on the couch, my head resting on his shoulder. Outside, the rising wind slanted snow across the window.

"Sukie was three years younger than me," David said. "She used to tag along wherever I went. God, she was so beautiful. Half my friends were in love with her. When . . . it . . . happened, Dad sent me a telegram." He paused, reliving the moment. "Have you ever thought, when something terrible happens, 'a moment ago things were not like this; let it be then, not now, anything but now'? And you try to remake then, but you know you can't?"

Tears stung my eyelids. I couldn't speak.

"Anyway," David said wearily, "I got here as quickly as I could, but I was working on a project literally in the middle of nowhere and it took a few days to get back. By then the funeral was over."

I remembered the lilies I had seen in the woods and the ones he had laid on her grave. At least when my men died, I thought, I was there to say goodbye.

"Is your family in Kingsport, then?" I asked.

David shook his head. "Concord. My folks went back right after the funeral. Somehow, my mother has managed to persuade herself that Sukie's murder was God's will. Tracey's death was part of some divine plan. She's retreated into a kind of religious stupor, dragging Dad to church with her all the time. It's one of those places where they do a lot of wailing and chanting. Dad just follows her like some kind of zombie. I don't know, I guess if it helps them deal with the pain, it's okay. At least they have each other, and their God, whoever he is, to cling to. It's Ian I'm really worried about. My brother-in-law. He was devastated by the murders, but what's been going on in the press since is beyond bearing."

"The 'Susie' articles?" I asked.

"Those, and the centerfold pictures. Ian never knew that Sukie posed for those. She didn't see any harm in a few nude pictures and the money just about put her through college. But Ian's pretty much of a straight arrow and she let him believe she'd made it through with waitressing and a small scholarship. Seeing her like that on the covers of magazines, hearing people talk, it's killing him. He's afraid it's all people will remember about her, that maybe they'll think she was some cheap tramp who got what she deserved."

David's arm lay across my shoulders. I reached up and gently drew his hand down against my cheek, and kissed it. I wondered if he knew about the tape Ian Forrester had sent to my sister.

I asked how he had come to be part of the mock jury. "Obviously nobody knows you're Susan Forrester's brother, or they wouldn't have let you within a mile of Kerrin's office. Or the Reid's house, for that matter." I sat up suddenly, pushing away from him so that I could see his face. "You did that on purpose. You deliberately set out to meet Max so you could get yourself invited to the Party. Why did you do that?"

David's voice was cool, casual, hard. "I want to see that justice is done," he said.

CHAPTER TWENTY

On Monday morning, I took care of some of personal bookkeeping. The level of organization I maintained in my client's records didn't seem to apply to my own. As a result, it took me as long to pick my way through my little maze of bills and remittances as it did to sort out any of theirs, which was absurd considering the relative complexity of our affairs. I left the house at twelve-thirty, giving myself time to make a quick stop at the bank before meeting Dr. Natalie Reeve at one.

Though I hadn't consulted Natalie professionally for over two years, we still touched base every few months. She had been key to helping me deal with my mother's illness and, to a lesser extent, with the car crash. Even with her, I had been unable to open up completely about my feelings for Brian and Rory.

I always enjoyed our get-togethers, especially when we got together at Lotty's. Lotty cooked seafood like no one else could. For years, I had tried working my way through the menu but it was impossible; Lotty was constantly devising new recipes. The only thing that never changed was the clam chowder. If Lotty had ever tried to replace it with something else, she would have been lynched on the spot.

The restaurant was crowded. Natalie was already seated at a table in the far corner. She waved when she saw me, and the line of people waiting impatiently to indulge themselves reluctantly shuffled aside to let me pass.

I threaded my way around tables set with printed cloths and colored glassware. They were well spaced, which made life easy for the wait staff and gave customers at least the illusion of privacy. Halfway across the room, I noticed a group of teenaged girls, unremarkable except for the fact that one of them was Simone Outray. She glanced up as I passed and our eyes locked briefly. I smiled politely. She did not. But the dull flush of embarrassment on her cheeks told me she remembered where we'd met.

Natalie greeted me with a hug and said, "Well, don't you look great. Where did you get that fabulous sweater?"

We spent a half hour on soup and social niceties before the conversation swung, as it inevitably did these days, to the Outray case.

"I heard Kerrin's involved in that one," Natalie said. "I sure don't envy her."

She and Kerrin had trained together and, at one point, they had even talked about going into partnership, but then Brian had come along and Kerrin's focus had shifted away from clinical psychology.

I said, "What's your opinion of a defendant hiring a psychiatrist and pleading insanity or diminished capacity or whatever? Professionally, I mean."

Natalie is the sort of plump, fair, flyaway woman you expect to find baking brownies and running the PTA rather than counseling troubled teens for a living and rock climbing in her rare time off.

She shook her head at my question. "Criminal responsibility is never a medical call, Nina, it's a legal one. A psychiatrist goes into court to try to describe the defendant's state of mind at the time a crime was committed—though that's sort of like trying to reconstruct a dream you had the night before. Of course, the prosecution hires a different psychiatrist, who usually shoots her down. It's up to the jury to decide which one is more credible, and whether the person they're talking about is, in fact, responsible for the criminal act in question."

"But most jurors have no more medical background than I do," I objected. "How can they be expected to take complex medical testimony and apply the law to it?"

"That's the crux of the problem exactly. Can a lay jury reasonably settle a scientific argument? It's one thing if they're presented with a well-established organic illness, like epilepsy. But when you get into a more controversial diagnosis, like stunted emotional development or personality disorder, things get a lot more uncertain. The question always arises, has the defendant made this condition up in order to get away with murder? It makes a tough case for a lawyer to win. Which is why they turn to people like Kerrin for advice."

The waitress came over to clear plates and pour coffee. While Natalie added cream and sugar to hers, I said, "But aren't there some kind of tests to measure a person's mental health? Surely there must be some basic guidelines to follow in coming up with a diagnosis in the first place. It wasn't that tough to figure out Mom had Alzheimer's."

"No, in her case it wasn't." Natalie stirred her coffee. "And sure, there are tests in place for mental disorders. But you need someone to measure the test results and that's where you can get a lot of disagreement. I was at a conference a couple of weeks ago in New York. One of the key speakers was a forensic psychiatrist and the case study he presented included a diagnostic tool called the PET scan. Positron emission technology. It's a functional brain scan that gives you pictures of the activity in a living, working brain."

"What? How does that work?"

"Okay. You know that a brain requires glucose to function."

"Yeah," I said, smiling at the slab of chocolate cake the waitress reverently placed in the middle of our table. Natalie grinned and forked up an inelegant mouthful. I waited while she swallowed and dabbed her mouth with her napkin.

"So," she said. "You inject radioactive glucose into the subject, and the PET indicates where in the brain sugar is being used. If the pictures show decreased glucose use, then the brain is not functioning normally. Seems straightforward, right? The problem is, scientists are still trying to decide what the pictures they get actually reveal. I mean, how do you evaluate judgment or remorse or impulsiveness in a person?"

I said, "Maybe you can't measure them specifically, but isn't the decreased glucose use enough to determine that something is out of whack in the person's brain?"

Natalie pointed her fork at me. "You have just hit on the very point this psychiatrist was making. In his case study, he showed us the PET scans for two stroke victims. The pictures were nearly identical, which would lead you to expect that the clinical findings for the two people would also be similar, right? They'd have the same problems. In fact, they weren't even close. The one guy was paralyzed on his right side and had practically no speech. The other one looked clinically fine."

I nodded. "So even though the pictures indicated some kind of trauma or malfunction or whatever in the brain, it wasn't clear what the problem was."

"That's right."

"If you took that kind of evidence to court, you'd have experts on both sides arguing that it proved their case. In fact, all you'd be presenting the jury with is a scientific dispute."

Natalie said, "And as we all know, to a jury, conflict among the experts means a reasonable doubt. They're forced to err on the side of caution. So all the scientific evidence that should prove a case one way or the other ends up being used as nothing more than a prop to create confusion in the courtroom, rather than to clarify something technical."

I signaled the waitress for a coffee refill. "Aside from this PET scan aren't there any established tests that are more reliable? Less disputable?"

"Sure. But you have to remember that any kind of testing can be a double-edged sword. Any defense lawyer worth his salt is going to be pretty selective about it; he's only going to present the bits that are beneficial to his case. He's going to take his best shot at linking his client's mental disorder to the criminal act, preferably by establishing some kind of pattern of behavioral abnormality, and the psychiatrist is going to provide him with the bullets. But the lawyer has to be careful, because test results that 'prove' a mental disorder could also indicate potential future dangerousness. Is dangerousness a word? Anyway, you know what

I mean."

"Yeah, I'm afraid I do. Both sides get so preoccupied with scoring points that somehow the facts get lost."

Natalie gave me a look I recognized from my sessions in her office. "Are you worried about Kerrin in this case," she asked, "Or something else?"

"Kerrin," I said. "And something else."

"Want to talk about it?"

I shook my head.

"So what's new?" she said. "You've got my number. Use it if you need an ear. I've got to run. I've got a patient at two-thirty."

It was my turn to pick up the check, so Natalie hurried off to her appointment while I settled in to one more cup of coffee and a mental debate over the remaining hunk of cake, which my bad angel won with the argument that I never eat dessert at home.

Guilt sharpened the edge of pleasure as I spooned up the rich dark chocolate. I was savoring the last delicious mouthful when Simone Outray flopped down in the chair Natalie had vacated.

Without preamble she said, "What were you talking to her about?"

After her behavior at the Party, neither her rudeness nor her abrupt question came as much of a shock. I said merely, "Her, who?"

"Dr. Reeve."

"That's none of your business."

"You were talking about me, weren't you? Why? Did *she* hire you to spy on me?"

"What the . . . " I set my coffee cup very carefully back in its saucer. "Look, Simone," I said, trying to keep my voice even. "I don't know what you're talking about. Dr. Reeve is a friend of mine. We were having lunch, that's all. I didn't know you two knew each other, I don't know who *she* is,"—though I thought I could hazard a guess—"And, frankly, I don't want to know."

Simone sat stiffly opposite, radiating rage. I was beginning to wish Natalie hadn't left. She would know how to handle this, how to defuse the hostility that was backed up like a sewer in this girl. Simone had to be one of Natalie's patients. Nothing else could explain the girl's anxiety at seeing us together. She stared at me for a moment longer then slumped abruptly in her chair, like a puppet whose strings have been cut, as she accepted the truth of what I was saying.

She was wearing a thin gold bracelet on her right wrist and she began to turn it, straightening a kink in the chain. "You don't know what it's like," she mumbled. "Nobody does. Not even Dr. Reeve. It's all so awful, and I just don't know what to do."

She looked on the verge of tears. I stared at her helplessly, wishing myself anywhere but there. "Simone, I'm not . . ."

A tear slid down the girl's cheek and she raised an impatient hand to brush it away. Her tone hardened. "Oh, what the hell. What difference does any of it make? Nothing ever changes anyway and it never ends."

She pushed away from the table and got up. I opened my mouth to say something, but the waitress appeared at my elbow with the bill and an offer of yet more coffee, and by the time she fluttered off, Simone was gone.

CHAPTER TWENTY-ONE

"Goddamn it!" Mel Deloitte hurled a paperweight against the wall. It was heavy crystal and it shattered. The cleaning lady would be picking fragments out of the carpet for weeks.

I had stopped by on my way home from Lotty's, hoping to catch up on some paperwork. I had expected the lawyer to be in his downtown office and I was surprised to find him pacing his study in a fury.

He smoothed a hand over his hair, struggling for control. "That was a damn useless thing to do. Is it too early for brandy?"

In view of his performance with the paperweight, I thought I'd better pour. He emptied the snifter in one gulp.

"Okay," he said. "Damage control."

As Kerrin's sister and a member of the mock jury, my status with Deloitte had been upgraded from factotum to almost equal and he seemed to regard me as a member of the team. The damage he referred to was splashed across the front page of the *Daily Express*. He flapped the paper at me, inviting me to read the story.

It was not good journalism. The story was biased, emotional, and escaped being libelous only by its generous use of questions. Factual references were made to both the Kennedy Smith acquittal and the Menendez brothers' mistrial. It was noted that in the O.J. Simpson case, the attention of the court had been successfully diverted from murder and refocused on race issues. In detailing the case against Randy Outray, the author was careful to stick to the facts but even the most perverse reader could not fail to draw the intended conclusions.

"The stakes are high in this one, folks," he wrote. "If he is found guilty, Randy Outray faces the death penalty. But at Max and Sonja Reid's Christmas bash on Saturday night, he didn't look as though he had a care in the world. Could it be he knows something we don't?

Do heavyweight lawyer Mel Deloitte and his iron lady consultant Kerrin Adams have the muscle for a knockout?"

The article reduced a murder trial to a spectator sport whose outcome seemed as predictable as a staged wrestling match. In terms of rallying support to the victim, nothing could have been more effective. No sentimental biographies or gruesome murder scene photos would engender the same outrage and hostility as the gossipy sports motif. The unsubtle allusion that the rules of the game were different for rich players would only add fuel to the fire.

The sidebar made my stomach ache. Throughout were echoes of my confidences to David Maitland. I couldn't believe he'd shared them with a reporter but where else could the information have come from? A players' roster of the defense team highlighted Deloitte's—and half the state judiciary's—membership at the Clubbe, speculated on steam room "negotiations" and, most painfully for me, gave a bio of Kerrin that pondered the hardening effects of personal tragedy. Far from being sympathetic, it lambasted her for heartlessness. I could just imagine her reaction.

As if on cue, the front door banged open and Kerrin stormed in waving a rolled-up newspaper in Deloitte's face.

"Have you seen this?" she demanded. "I found it on my doorstep, with my name underlined in red."

Carefully, I folded the paper I had been reading and placed it in the middle of Deloitte's desk. Belatedly, Kerrin noticed me.

"What are you doing here?"

"I work here. At least, part of the time."

"Have you seen this?"

I nodded.

"It has to be that damned Ian Forrester again."

Deloitte raised an eyebrow. "Again?"

So Kerrin hadn't told him about the videotape after all. From her initial reaction, I'd expected her to rush right down to the courthouse and file an injunction, but she had let it go. She wouldn't this time.

"It's defamatory," she raged. "What does my private life have to do with anything?"

"It's no worse than what the *Barker* printed about Susan Forrester," I pointed out.

Kerrin rounded on me. "What the hell do you mean? I'm not on trial here, nor is Mel. And so far, neither is Randy Outray. The *Daily Express* has no business trying this case in print before it even gets to court."

I shook my head in amazement at her attitude. "Sorry, Kerrin, that argument won't wash with me. You haven't said boo about all the defamatory comments that have been leveled at Susan Forrester in the papers, and she shouldn't be on trial at all. She was the victim."

Deloitte eyed me narrowly. "Just whose side are you on here, Nina?"

"I don't have a 'side', Mel," I said. "I can see what you're thinking: Nina's on the mock jury, she was at the Reid's. Maybe she planted the story. You know, I almost wish I had. It was insufferably arrogant of Randy Outray to be out partying on Saturday night. Don't you think, as his legal counsel, you should have advised him against it?"

"I did," Deloitte muttered. "He wouldn't listen. You've got to understand, Nina, people like the Outrays, they have no sense of limitation. Anything they want to do is okay because they're the ones doing it."

"Lèse majesté?"

Deloitte shrugged.

"And is that what happened with Susan and Tracey Forrester? Randy Outray felt like murdering them, so he did?"

Deloitte said nothing. Kerrin looked impassive.

I waited for her to say something, anything, to reaffirm my loyalty to her. Nothing but a slowly widening silence followed me out the door.

*

Feeling too restless to go home and mindful of the chocolate cake, I took the Sanderson's dogs to the ravine and let them off their leads while I jogged. The crisp air energized them. Caleb and Kelsey lunged through the fluffy drifts like puppies, snuffling excitedly at unimaginable scents. Sighting what appeared to be an especially deep, downy pile, Caleb bounded away in a graceless rush and dove into it head first. Hanna Barbera would have made much of the moment. The dog lay flat out while, in gentle slow motion, snow slid down the face of the rock it had hidden and dropped in a cloud onto his back. I laughed out loud. From under his snowdrift, Caleb gave me a baleful look. Canine pride had suffered a blow. The dog picked himself up, shook out his coat, and stalked away with as much dignity as he could muster.

The woods had a silvery, quiet look. Sunshine glimmered through ice crystals in the air and glinted off crusted tree limbs. Mine were the first human tracks on the path. When I was small, Kerrin always took me out in fresh fallen snow to make angels. I walked behind her, carefully fitting my own small boots into her larger footprints, pretending she was King Wenceslas and I was the page. Whenever she said "here!" the two of us fell giggling to the ground, waving our arms and legs. Some days we left whole flights of angels in our wake.

My instinctive reaction to the criticism of my sister in the *Express* had been defensive. It had hurt to see our private tragedy so publicly displayed. But Kerrin herself had quashed my sympathy, and her outrage reminded me that a relative stranger moved behind the familiar facade. The character I had assigned her so many years ago was of my own imagining; I had already learned that lesson.

On the path ahead, Kelsey nosed at a set of rabbit tracks. She must have decided they were too old to be worth pursuing because she only followed them for a step or two before abandoning the scent and running on. We had reached the half-way point in the loop, the spot where two months ago yellow crime scene tape had marked a murder scene. The tape was gone now, the birch trees gray skeletons against the sky. I thought of the woman and the little girl who had died on that spot, beauty and innocence, gone from a world that seemed content to let such things run through its fingers like water. I thought about Simone Outray's bitter outbursts and of the pain in David Maitland's voice when he talked about his sister. I felt old loyalties shift like sand beneath my feet.

There was a movement in the bushes at the edge of the clearing, then a soft plop as a clump of snow was dislodged from a branch. I jerked around to see who was there, heart thudding, mind all at once full of nameless terrors.

It was only the rabbit. He had been joined by a friend and the two of them froze, noses quivering, when they saw me. I let out a breath I hadn't realized I was holding. The sound alarmed the animals into retreat and they vanished back into the brush like clumsy ghosts.

I was shivering, though not with cold. I whistled the dogs to me and snapped on their leads. We had come far enough; it was time to go home.

CHAPTER TWENTY-TWO

The library was crowded. High school kids were doing homework and socializing in roughly equal proportion. It would be a while before a computer terminal came free and I needed to access the library's archives. What I wanted I didn't think I could find from the comfort of my home, though Brent William might have been able to point me in the right direction.

As I waited, I thumbed through a copy of Harris's *History of Kingsport*. I didn't hold out much hope of finding the answers I was looking for there. Or anywhere, really. Could anything, any fact or hint from the past, anything in the history of the Outray family, confirm a dysfunction severe enough to explain Randy's grotesque act? If so, I needed to find it myself, without courtroom rhetoric or legal hyperbole. Otherwise, I couldn't remain part of Kerrin's mock jury. Whatever loyalty I felt toward my sister could not outweigh the abhorrence I felt for her client.

According to Harris, the founding fathers of Kingsport, Jeremiah Outray among them, had fled various parts of Europe for the new world, where a combination of brains, brawn and ambition had resulted in fortunes in gunpowder, oil, railroads, and lumber. It was interesting to note where the boldness and drive that had led its original settlers to prosperity had dwindled in a few generations to complacency. Where Jeremiah and his sons had exerted themselves to create new lives, their grandsons had felt less compulsion to labor. By the end of the Second World War, the family holdings were so extensive that perhaps it seemed beside the point to do anything more than simply enjoy them.

I slid the book back onto the shelf just as a kid with the body of a football player and a mouth full of jumbled teeth quitted the desk I had been waiting for. I commandeered the vacant seat an instant before a pouty blonde slid into it and called up the database I was looking for. I would start with John and Zoe Outray.

There seemed nothing remarkable in either of their early lives. Both had gone to the usual schools, with the usual results, had "come out" with the usual fanfare and gone on to sit on various boards and committees. I glossed over long descriptions of houses, yachts, horses, clothes, jewelry, wedding, wedding presents, and wedding guests. The birth of a son after five years of marriage had been heralded as a major achievement. Great things were predicted for the future of this golden boy; the women's magazines had fairly cooed over images of the angelic cherub and his stunning mother. Simone's arrival six years later had been acknowledged with much less hoopla, which may have been unjust but was hardly surprising. Having fulfilled her duty by producing a perfect heir to the family name, Zoe had already moved on to the next stage of her life, as benefactress to various charitable concerns.

There were the usual clips of the family on holiday, skiing at Aspen, sunning in Hawaii. Running the pictures together like a slide show, it was fascinating to see the development of the Outray children. Simone did not share her brother's good looks but there was something in the bone structure of her face that could, if allowed, have lent her character and a kind of grace. Given her mother's wide-eyed, smooth skinned elegance, I was surprised that so little effort seemed to have been taken with the daughter. But it was clear, skimming through the passage of years, that the mother had gradually distanced herself from her second child. Randy, looking the epitome of the spoiled little rich kid, was at the forefront of most of the pictures; Simone stood on the fringes. I wondered which had come first, the chill and disenchantment of Zoe's worldly sophistication, or Simone's lack of warmth. Perhaps there was ice on both sides, and one had merely reinforced the other.

The Outrays lived their lives on quite a different plane than I did and the constant run of social engagements made me wonder if they ever spent a quiet evening at home, as a family. On the whole, I thought not. Randy and Simone were given over to the care of a succession of nannies, sent to the right schools and taken on the right holidays. There was some mention of The Loftwood School, which surprised me, as it was a parochial school with a reputation for spartan living conditions and harsh discipline. Moreover, it was a girls' school. Randy might have benefitted from such restraint but I would have thought his sister too susceptible to its rigid morality. Maybe that was where she had acquired the expression of permanent disapproval with which she seemed to view the world.

I had, I suppose, expected to find some evidence of a domineering father, a demanding mother, of goals being set for the son that were impossible to reach. Instead, I found over-indulgence and great wealth allied to an almost total lack of purpose. In trying to reconcile that history with the murder in the woods, I could only think of Leopold and Loeb, two young men who, for no other reason than to see what it would feel like, killed a fourteen-year old boy with as little compunction as they might have felt in stepping on an ant. I didn't care what a psychiatrist might make of that. Pitiable though it might be for anyone to be so totally without conscience, as far as I was concerned, there was no possible excuse for such an action, nor any hope of redemption.

*

It was almost dark by the time I left the library. On the way home, I wandered over to the corner to see if Yuri was roasting chestnuts today. People hustled past with the preoccupied air of those who know exactly how few shopping days were left until Christmas. Shopkeepers kept extended store hours in order to accommodate those with lists more extensive than mine.

It had been a very busy day, Yuri apologized, but if I was not in too much of a hurry, he would heat a new batch of chestnuts just for me. While I waited, I studied the display at Irina's newsstand. The usual atrocities in Africa and the Middle East competed for attention with the diet secrets of the rich and famous. Aliens had been spotted in Montana; a woman in California had just given birth to triplets, each of whom was a different color; and the CIA was plotting to put a new tsar on the Russian throne.

"This one ought to appeal to you," I told Irina.

"Perhaps," she answered gravely, "they will make Yuri Tsar."

I laughed. "Will you ever go back to Russia, do you think?"

Irina shook her head. "There is nothing for me there."

"No family? Brothers or sisters?"

"No. I had only one sister and she is gone, many years ago. She was sent to labor camp."

"Why?"

"She was poet. Nineteen-year old poet. An enemy of the people."

Fifty years hadn't eased the pain. "You still miss her."

"She is still my sister," Irina said simply.

*

It was dark when I got home. There was a message from David, canceling our dinner date. He sounded hurried and distracted and I tried hard not to mind.

A pile of documents littered the harvest table. Brent William had dropped off copies of his business plan, budget projections, market analysis, all the groundwork for "Roadblocks." I had agreed to go over it for him and give him a formal assessment.

I opened a bottle of wine and got out some crackers and spinach dip. I plugged in my iPod, shut the blinds, and straightened the pillows on the couch. I penciled a note in the margin of Brent's outline, trying to give his work the attention it deserved while Robbie Williams crooned in the background. There was a lot of information to wade through. Brent had been very thorough.

The music shifted to an instrumental arrangement of the love song from a film about a doomed love affair. Something in its muted melancholy found too ready an echo in me. I reached over and turned it off.

I felt tired and depressed. Too much had happened in the last few weeks and the pleasant things had somehow faded back out of mind, leaving me with an oddly flattened feeling.

I knew what it was. I had lived with loneliness a long time. It was something that was always there. I had learned to accept it, even—sometimes—to enjoy it, but on evenings like this one, the desperate self-sufficiency I had contrived was not quite enough.

I tuned in to Radio Kingsport. Red Reilly's late night phone-in lines were jammed. The subject was vigilante justice. The callers were more pro than con and they based many of their comments on what they read in the *Express*.

I turned off the radio and turned on the TV for the eleven o'clock news. Outside the Outray estate, thirty-five women and a handful of men marched under a banner that read: "Join the Clubbe. Get away with murder."

At nine-thirty, a scuffle had broken out between a few of the marchers and the security guards John Outray had hired to disperse them. In the confusion, one of the side gates to the property had been left unattended. A dozen protesters had swarmed the house, hurling eggs and oaths in roughly equal proportion. It took the guards, aided by the police, almost an hour to round up all the troublemakers and take down their names. News at Eleven had coverage of the incident and the commentator sounded almost gleeful as she identified Ian Forrester in the crowd. He had the dead eyes of a zombie. With a shock, I recognized David beside him, tugging at his arm and trying to pull him out of camera range.

It wasn't until a little after two a.m. that one of the guards patrolling the Outray garden noticed the door to the indoor pool was ajar. A few minutes later, he discovered the body of Randy Outray floating face down in the shallow end. He had been shot in the back.

CHAPTER TWENTY-THREE

"What a very dark horse your David turned out to be," Sonja Reid said archly. "It's rather exciting in a way to think of him being here, practically *stalking* young Randy Outray right in my own living room."

We were sitting in her library sorting out the last of the Party accounts, my own included. Without its masses of flowers and the glittering panoply of the Christmas ball, the house looked overexposed. The only remaining concession to the season was a perfectly symmetrical tree, trimmed in gold, coldly elegant in the curve of the main staircase.

For Sonja, the drama of having an accused murderer in her home had been overshadowed by the thrill of having brought him face to face—maybe—with his killer. It hadn't taken the police long to sort out who David was. Everyone involved in the demonstration had been questioned. No one had been arrested because no weapon had been found and so far, the police had only circumstantial evidence pointing to potential suspects. The suspects it pointed to most strongly were Ian Forrester and David Maitland.

Predictably, Kerrin was furious when she learned who David was and she wasted no time in telling me so.

"What the hell did you think you were playing at?" she had screamed, ignoring the distraction of the coffee mug I waved at her. "No wonder the *Express* knew so much about the case we were preparing."

Resolutely, I filled my own mug, cradling its reassuring warmth in my hands. I said, "I didn't know what David's involvement was until after the Reid's party. And then I sort of figured it was up to him to tell you himself. Why did you invite him to be on the mock jury anyway? You didn't know him from a hole in the ground."

"Mel recommended him. He'd worked with him on some deal or other and when Maitland said he was going to be in town for a while, it seemed like a gift—someone totally outside the community, with no preconceived biases either way in the case." She threw up her hands. "Not that we need a case anymore. The goddamn defendant is dead."

"And you think David is responsible for that?"

"He may not have pulled the trigger, but he must have known what was in his brother-in-law's mind. Either way, he's guilty."

"I don't believe it."

"What?"

"He wouldn't take the law into his own hands like that," I said, wondering if my words sounded as false as they felt. Much as I wanted to believe they were true, I couldn't dodge the memory of David, saying in that hard little voice, "I want to see that justice is done."

Admittedly, where men were concerned, my instincts were more than a little rusty. How well did I know David, after all?

Kerrin said, "He probably knew who *you* were, all along. You made the perfect conduit for him. Why else would he have hit on you?"

Why else, indeed.

Something of what I was feeling must have shown on my face, because Kerrin said quickly, "I didn't mean it like that, Nina. It's just, knowing who he is now, the whole thing looks so contrived. Surely you can see that."

I didn't answer.

Kerrin's mouth tightened. Her voice wavered a little. "You know, Nina, sometimes it's a whole lot easier to think that you're in love, than to accept that you're alone," she said.

There was no point in arguing. It would have been a very odd Cinderella indeed who could have ventured out of the dreary seclusion of my life, into contact with David's particular brand of warmth and humor, without something of the sort happening. But even if he wasn't Prince Charming, I wasn't prepared to jettison him without a hearing.

Sonja's voice intruded on my reverie. She was nattering on about her other guests in a way that left no doubt they had been only a backdrop for her centerpiece, the Outrays. Sonja invariably built any social function around personalities. It was no wonder she had been so nervous beforehand; if the Outrays had failed to attend, her soiree would have been just another fancy dress party.

"You spent quite a bit of time with Simone," Sonja said. Her tone invited confidences. "Tell me, what did you think of her? Isn't she just too pathetic for words?"

"Actually, I did feel rather sorry for her," I said. "It must be a very difficult time for all of them."

"Oh, sure. But the rest of the family seems to be handling it with so much more . . . style. Of course, Simone has always been the odd duck in that group. She is so very *ordinary*."

I said drily, "Being ordinary is not a heinous sin."

"Oh," Sonja said, "Don't you think so?"

I concentrated fiercely on the bills in front of me, aware of Sonja's speculative gaze and trying to ignore it. After a few minutes, I got twitchy and said, "Is there something you wanted?"

"Nooo, not exactly."

She drew one long, red fingernail slowly across the cover of the book she was holding. Judging by the thickness and the color of the dust jacket, it was Grisham's *The Chamber*, which I had seen lying on the hall table when I came in. "I just wondered, Nina, how well you actually know this David Maitland. I mean, you seemed very chummy the other night. He must have let something slip." She paused expectantly.

"Not a thing," I said firmly. "I had no idea he had any connection at all to the Forresters."

"Well, have you talked to him since . . . ?"

"Since the party?"

"Don't be obtuse," she said impatiently. "You know very well what I mean. Since Randy Outray was found murdered."

"No," I said.

"Do you think he did it? Or Ian Forrester?"

My voice sounded stiff to my own ears. "As far as I know, there's nothing to indicate that this murder is related to the Forresters."

"Oh, don't be naive, my dear. It would be just too, too coincidental that those two were hanging around the Outray's house along with that gang waving their ridiculous posters about the Clubbe and then Randy gets murdered while they're there? Please, dear, for your own sake, take *off* the blinders."

I didn't want to. I wanted to go on blind and instinct-driven. But as I sat there at Sonja Reid's mahogany desk, with its tooled leather top and its gold border etching, the thing that I had been trying to keep back, dammed out of mind, broke over me. I had already spent a sleepless night staring dry-eyed at the ceiling, going over and over everything that had happened since David had entered the scene. I told myself that everything he had said and done could bear an innocent interpretation as well as a guilty one. A word here, a look there. Never did frailer witnesses plead their case more desperately. And the night of the Party . . . but here memory whirled into such ragged confusion that I felt like Alice in Wonderland lost in a flurry of playing cards. I wondered if I would be forced yet again to put memories away in a drawer, like cards, taking them out at intervals to thumb over in a dreary game of solitaire.

*

There was no message from David when I got home and no answer at the number he had given me. To fill the void, I did some busywork: dusting, laundry, vacuuming. The thought of scrubbing floors was too much, so I tried David's number again, still with no reply.

He was staying at the Forrester's, that much I knew. He had told me how concerned he was for Ian's emotional stability and I suspected that he had only participated in the demonstration in order to keep a weather eye on his brother-in-law. I could only hope David hadn't lost track of him long enough for Ian to have shot Randy Outray.

About the other possibility, I didn't want to think at all.

The weather had been unexpectedly warm all day. Now it was cooling again, and the night air was still, held in a pall of mist. I could hear the occasional soft drip of moisture from the boughs that overhung my roof. Restlessly, I wandered around the apartment, feeling strangely anxious and afraid. Never before had I felt the lack of a friend so keenly.

On my third pass through the living room, I came to a decision. This time, I was not going to wait for bad news come to me.

Pulling on my boots, I grabbed my coat and headed out.

*

Ian Forrester's house was one of a dozen on a key-shaped street that backed onto the ravine. Though the survey was relatively new, enough of the original trees had been left standing that it already looked well established. I drove slowly, trying to make out numbers among twinkle lights and flashing Santas. In the end, it was easy to spot which house must be Ian's. It was the only one in the key without Christmas decorations of any kind. His was a two-story house of fieldstone and siding, with large bow windows on either side of the front door. The porch light was not on, but lamplight glowed from somewhere at the back of the house. I paused at the front door, studying the beveled glass in the fanlight as I tried to screw up my courage to knock. When I finally did, the door was answered almost immediately by a tall, gaunt man in a bathrobe and slippers.

He looked startled at the sight of me and I saw his gaze shift to a point somewhere beyond my shoulder, as though he had been expecting someone else. He shook his head, muttered something that sounded like "no interviews" and started to shut the door.

"Mr. Forrester?" I said quickly, placing my hand on the door to keep it open. "I'm sorry to disturb you. My name is Nina Ryan. I'm a friend of David's. Is he here? Could I speak to him for a minute, please?"

"A friend of David's?" he repeated dully.

"That's right. Is he here just now?"

Ian Forrester shook his head. "No. He went out to get something. I thought it was . . . I thought you were him, coming back. Maybe he forgot his key."

I swallowed hard. "Do you know how long he'll be? I can wait."

Something flickered in his eyes as he tried to deal with the thought, and I was sharply reminded of my mother in the days when she still had the strength to fight against the darkness overtaking her.

"You're not a reporter?" he said.

"No. I'm not a reporter, I promise. I'm a friend of David's."

Ian nodded slowly and stepped away from the door, leaving me to close it and follow him down the hall to the family room and the light I had seen from outside.

It was a comfortable room of generous proportions, with lots of built-in cupboards, and shelves crammed with paperbacks. The walls above the wainscoting had been painted deep red; the rugs and furniture were dark green, with accents of the same rusty shade. Despite the lack of seasonal trimming, it looked oddly festive. In the daytime, sunlight would pour through the sliding glass doors that led to a deck outside. The doors, and the windows that flanked them on the left, looked directly into the ravine where Susan and Tracey Forrester had been murdered. I wondered how Ian could bear it.

Someone, probably a cleaning lady, was keeping the house immaculate. There was no dust on the tables, no clutter in the kitchen. The only thing out of place was the jumble of photographs on the mantle. Their frames looked smudged with handling. Two white roses drooped in a bud vase beside them.

In the summer before she died, I had taken my mother for rambling walks along the river. Once, I had bent to gather a few wildflowers, thinking they would make a cheerful nosegay for her room. But she had cried out at me to stop. "Please let them live," she had said. "Cut flowers die so slowly. Like me." Without his family, I thought, the man in front of me was dying slowly, too.

Forrester shuffled across to the trestle table behind the couch. His hands groped over the objects on it as though he were blind, fumbling past the lamp, moving softly over the clock, fingering a magazine, until, finally, his fingers touched a tumbler half-full of amber liquid.

I said, "Ian."

He turned. He had lifted the tumbler as if to drink from it, and across the rim, his eyes met mine. With his back to the lamp, his face was a pale blur, his eyes dark and expressionless. As I looked at him, bewildered, and beginning to be frightened, I suddenly understood. Goose-pimple cold slid ghost-handed over my skin. I was gripping the back of a chair; without it, I think I would have fallen.

I said hoarsely, "Ian."

He took no notice. He put the tumbler down and turned toward the patio doors. Lamplight rippled along the folds of his robe; it caught his face and gleamed back from eyes as wide and glassy as a doll's.

I said, "Ian, answer me. Did you kill Randy Outray?"

The fixed eyes never moved, but he gave a queer little sigh. The obsessive question burst from me. "Did David help you?"

Ian's head inclined toward me. I repeated the question urgently. "Did he?"

It wouldn't work. The broken man in front of me was going to keep his secrets locked inside. In despair, I watched him fumble with the lock and slide open the door to the deck. He drifted outside to stand at the rail overlooking the ravine.

CHAPTER TWENTY-FOUR

I heard the front door open and shut. The bolt sliding home. Footsteps in the hall. Keys tossed onto the kitchen counter. Then a startled exclamation.

"Nina?"

Still gripping the back of the chair for support, I turned to face David. Hot tears stained my cheeks but I made no move to wipe them away.

David looked haggard, his eyes hard as stones. There were lines in his face that I hadn't seen there before.

"Where's Ian?"

His voice sounded strained and I heard a blaze of anger licking through it that he didn't trouble to suppress.

The question was answered by Ian himself. In a slow turn, he retreated from the middle of the deck to the far side. David lifted his head sharply and I followed his look in time to see Ian melt into the shadows like a wraith.

David took the space between us in two strides, his leap out of immobility so sudden that I reacted without reason, a blind thing in a panic, releasing my hold on the chair and putting out futile hands to break the tempest.

David stopped dead.

"I see," he said.

So did I. I had seen even as doubt reacting on fear had driven me to raise my hands against him. Now they dropped slowly back to my sides. I couldn't speak.

I began to cry again, not desperately or tragically, but silently and without hope, the tears spilling raggedly over my cheeks and my face ugly with crying.

I felt David move past me to the sliding doors, heard him say something to Ian. He didn't look at me as he guided his brother-in-law up the stairs to the second floor. Ian moved stiffly, like an old man, David murmuring encouragement at his elbow.

I should have gone then. Instead, I moved to the table where Ian Forrester had left the tumbler of brandy. I drank it with appreciation but no respect; it was the effect and not the drink that I craved.

In the kitchen, I splashed cold water on my face, effectively removing the traces of tears and the makeup I had so carefully applied before I left home. I noticed that the telephone had been unplugged from the wall, and I remembered that, when he answered the door, Ian had been worried I might be a reporter. I could imagine the hell they had created for him, asking the kind of questions that wreck lives and sell ten thousand extra copies.

When David came back downstairs, I was pulling the drapes across the windows.

David said, "Ian insists on having them open all the time. He stands for hours just staring out there. Thinking about . . . what happened."

The weariness in his voice made me wince. I forced myself to look at him. I clung to the drapery in my hand as I mustered the courage to say what had to be said.

"I'm sorry, David. I'm so sorry."

I was crushing the fabric I held. Carefully, I flattened it back out, ironing the creases between my palms.

"I know it isn't exactly—adequate—to tell someone you're sorry you suspected him of murder. But I am. I'm sorry I even let it cross my mind. And that was all it did, I swear it."

He stood, head down, like a beaten animal. "The police think I did it. They could see when they let us go this morning that Ian couldn't possibly have managed it. And I'm their next logical suspect. It's no secret I wanted Randy Outray dead."

I must have made some sound of protest because he looked up at me then.

"Do you really think I would have shot him?" he said.

"No, David."

A small tired smile glimmered through his beard. He looked at the empty glass on the table and a hint of the old amusement sounded in his voice. "Have you been raiding Ian's liquor cabinet?"

"It was already poured when I got here. I could do with a refill, though."

He got one for me and poured a generous glass for himself. We settled on the couch, close enough to touch, but not touching.

"Has he seen a doctor?" I asked.

"Oh, sure, for all the good it did. He tried to tough it out at first, but with all the publicity and everything, he just couldn't cope. He wasn't sleeping, he wasn't eating, hell, he wasn't even keeping himself clean. I made him go to the family doctor, a guy named Morris. He knew Susan and Tracey. I thought he'd be able to understand Ian's . . . problem. Morris gave him a prescription for some stuff to help him relax and told me to try to keep the pressure off as much as possible. I got a cleaning lady in, arranged for someone to cook meals. I make sure Ian has a shower in the morning. I see that he shaves. I keep hoping he'll spring around but the poor bastard just keeps sinking lower and lower. The doctor thinks I should have him committed 'to care,' whatever the hell that means."

"How did he end up at that rally?"

David snorted in disgust. "Half a dozen different outfits have been hitting on him ever since the girls were murdered. They call themselves 'active interest' groups. They all have catchy names and a particular cause they're beating the drum over. I've been trying to keep them away from him. You saw him, he's in no shape to take an active interest in anything. Those people are only interested in trading on his name." David sighed. "When they came around to the house last night, I was in the shower. I got downstairs just in time to see some guy helping Ian into a van. I high-tailed it after them and we all ended up at the Outrays."

David paused to take a sip of brandy. "A bunch of them were already there, out front. They scooped Ian up like he was the prize at a pig-calling contest. It took me a while to persuade them to let me anywhere near him and by the time they did, someone had called the cops."

I nodded. "That's the part they showed on TV."

"How did I look? They say the camera adds ten pounds."

"Not to worry."

He leaned forward to the brandy bottle and splashed some more into our glasses.

"What happened then?" I asked.

"People were running around all over the place. They sort of herded us over to one side, and every time they dragged someone else off the property, they added him—actually, most of them were 'hers'—to the pack. This one cop started asking everyone for ID, ladies first. I felt like I was back in school, you know? There'd be a fight in the hall or something and there was always one teacher 'taking names' for the principal. It was like that. Eventually, the cop got around to us. Ian didn't have any identification on him. I left the house in such a hurry, I didn't have any either. So they put us in a squad car and took us down to the police station and made us swear out affidavits telling them who we were. Checked our references. They were a little worried about Ian. He wasn't tracking too well and they wanted to make sure the drugs he was taking were prescription. They suggested that being anywhere near the Outrays was not smart. Just as they were about to send us home, the bulletin came in about Randy. I can't say I was sorry to hear it."

"What about Ian? Does he understand what's going on?"

David shook his head. "I don't think so. All the publicity, the 'Susie' articles and everything, have worn him down."

A spasm crossed his face. "I can't help feeling partly responsible. When I got here, I just wanted to do something, you know? Anything. Whatever I could to get this guy that had murdered my sister and her child. Ian was a little shaky, I could see that, but I had no idea how bad . . . I shouldn't have told him what went on with that mock jury."

"Was Ian the source for that story in the *Express*?" I asked.

"I don't know. Maybe. Probably. Reporters are constantly at him. I'm not here all the time. He could have done it. More likely he was persuaded to do it. I'm not sure he can form the intention to do anything himself anymore." David rubbed his face with one hand. "Maybe Dr. Morris is right, I should have him committed somewhere where they could help him. God knows, I'm not doing him any good."

I leaned forward and cupped David's face in my hand. He turned his head so his mouth was touched my palm.

"What happens now?" I asked. "You said the police think you shot him, but they haven't charged you with anything."

"Not yet, but they'd like to. It's a little tough without any evidence, though. Until they find a weapon or a witness or something, all they have is suspicion. It won't surprise me if they show up tomorrow with a search warrant for this house but until they get one, they'll have to make do with following me."

"What!"

He beckoned me to follow him into the darkened living room. Floral print toppers in some heavy material that probably matched the sofa curved over its top but the window itself was covered only by sheer drapery. I peered out.

My car stood where I had left it in the drive, with David's now tucked neatly in beside it. The right-hand side of the road looked deserted but two doors along on the left, I could make out the black outline of a sedan of some sort. Whoever was in it was smoking a cigarette. He'd left the window on the driver's side slightly open at the top and as I watched, he flicked a glowing stub out into the street.

I felt David very close behind me.

"What's he waiting for?"

David shrugged. "For me to do something incriminating, I guess. I noticed the car there earlier in the day but I didn't think anything of it at the time. Then when I went out to get Ian's prescription refilled, he followed me to the drug store, and home again, and I suspect he's planning to stay the night." He flashed me a look. "By now, he'll have run your plate."

"What for? I haven't done anything!"

"You're consorting with a suspect in a murder case."

"Consorting?"

"Just like Bonnie and Clyde."

"God, I hope not," I said. "Remember what happened to them."

As we padded back to the kitchen, David paused at the foot of the stairs, listening for a minute to reassure himself that all was quiet on the floor above.

"Does he sleepwalk?" I said.

David frowned. "It isn't sleepwalking exactly," he said. "He's conscious when he does it, at least as conscious as he ever gets these days. He just wanders around like he's looking for something and can't remember where he put it."

I made a sympathetic sound. "My Mom did that. It used to scare me to death because she wouldn't stay in the house. Twice I had to call the police. The neighbors were great, though. After the second time, they formed a 'Maggie Watch' to bring her home whenever she went out wandering."

David said, "Quite an emotional investment."

I shrugged. "Eventually you learn how to protect yourself."

"From?"

"Your feelings. You learn how not to have too many, so things don't bother you as much. The only trouble is, if you get really practiced at it, you tend to lose some of the good feelings, too. Let alone your ability to read other people's."

We were standing very close together. David slid his arms around me and tilted my face up to his. "Not to worry," he said. "You've done a pretty good job reading mine."

*

We were sitting at opposite ends of the couch, feet touching, and coffee cups instead of brandy glasses in our hands.

It was hard to escape the feeling that, with the death of Randy Outray, justice had been served, and a moral order, of a sort, restored. Had he died from lingering illness, or in the swift horror of an accident, I would have thought no further than that. But as long as the police suspected David of his murder, the ledger could not be closed. So, for over an hour, David and I had sifted through what we knew to be fact and what we dismissed as conjecture, from the time Susan and Tracey had met Randy Outray in the woods, to the moment he was discovered floating in his own swimming pool.

"It always comes back to motive," David said. "Who besides me had a strong enough motive to kill him?"

"What about some of the nutbars that were out parading in front of his house? One of them could have done it as easily as you."

"Vigilante justice?" David said doubtfully.

"Why not? It's no different from guys shooting doctors who perform abortions, or the neighborhood watch blowing up a crack house the police can't close down."

"I'd like to believe that. But, Nina, I have to tell you, those people out there were not like that. Their idea of a hostile act was throwing eggs on the windows, for God's sake. Besides, if any of them had had a gun, the police would have found it."

"They didn't find yours," I said.

He looked startled.

"What are you supposed to have done with it? Thrown it in the bushes, right? Well, that's exactly what one of the nutbars would have done, too. The police will find it, your fingerprints won't be on it, one of theirs will. End of story."

David looked unconvinced.

He said, "Don't most of these activist types want to advertise? What kind of statement can you make if you don't claim responsibility for the act?"

"Maybe they panicked. Maybe the reality of shooting someone didn't match the vision. I don't know. Who else could it have been?"

"Randy Outray was a psychotic son of a bitch. It wouldn't surprise me if people were standing in line to take a shot at him."

Snippets of gossip drifted into my mind; Sonja Reid hinting at past transgressions, telling me how Randy's family had bailed him out of trouble more than once before.

Had past trouble led to this present tragedy?

CHAPTER TWENTY-FIVE

The coffee we drank at midnight was no proof against the brandy. I fell asleep on the couch shortly afterward and woke there early in the morning, cozily tucked into a quilt David must have wrapped around me.

He was already up and showered. He offered to cook us both breakfast but I thought it best to leave before Ian or the cleaning lady put in an appearance.

The policeman outside had moved to the other side of the street. Whether it was in fact the same car and driver as the night before I didn't know and it didn't matter; his purpose hadn't altered.

The man's being there gave my departure an almost clandestine air that harkened back to high school days and illicit nights out. I felt torn between running for my car with my head down or thumbing my nose at the watcher. In the end, I did neither. David kissed me goodbye on the doorstep like a husband seeing his wife off to work and I drove off with only a passing glance at the man in the green car.

I went straight home. Before stepping into the shower, I put a pot of coffee on, so it was ready when I came back to the kitchen fifteen minutes later dressed in sweats and slippers. I drank the first mug while I toasted a bagel and laid my plans.

I am not a person who interferes readily in other people's lives. I have sat on the sidelines of my own too long to feel comfortable with a leading role in someone else's. One part of me insisted there was nothing to be done; no one would thank me for intervening in something that had nothing to do with me. Another part argued as strongly that whatever I could do for David must be done; his own hands were tied as much by Ian as the police. I sat at the harvest table, pushing crumbs around my plate and staring blindly into the sunshine streaming through the window. Sonja Reid's allusions to the past were all I had to go on, but maybe pulling on that thread would untangle the whole skein of trouble.

Decision brought a sense of relief so vivid it was almost physical. On the wave of it, I headed out to do some research.

I spent the day at the library, perusing the newspaper archives. Every so often, I had stopped reading long enough to print a copy of what was on the screen. Journalists had been circumspect in their reporting. Still, I picked up enough hints to piece together a couple of telling incidents.

Had I not known of Sonja's involvement in the Youth Development Project, I would have had no idea where to begin looking. As it was, it was easy. All I had to do was set a trace on the YDP. It led me soon enough to the kind of episode I was looking for. Due to the age of the participants, and, I supposed, the influence of the people involved, names were not often mentioned, but the insider information I had picked up over the years filled in the gaps and Sonja's bits of gossip didn't hurt.

I knew when Sonja had been named to the board of YDP. I vaguely remembered the hoopla over its inception. Two years ago or so, something had ruffled the feathers of Kingsport's upright city council. The details of whatever it was had been shuffled aside and forgotten amid the fanfare of the Project getting off the ground. It made sense to start my search a few months prior to that date, when funding would have been approved and reasons given for calling the Project into being.

Amid the usual political rhetoric, I found the reference I was looking for. It led me to a story that was buried before it got off the ground.

One fine summer morning, a young man (name withheld) had turned in a video to the police. He had rented it the night before from the Video Shoppe downtown, which stocks the usual run of romance and adventure flicks on its main shelves, and offers an eclectic assortment of erotica in the back room. The video in question had come from the back room. The young man had selected it, along with two others, on his way to a friend's stag party. There had been perhaps twenty guys at the party. By midnight, most of them were a little the worse for the beer they had consumed, but still game for the third and final feature of the night. The first two had been run of the mill films, short on plot and long on close ups of explicit sex between consenting partners of various persuasions. The third was entirely different.

It was an amateur effort, with no titles, no credits, and no soundtrack to speak of. Where the other movies boasted at least a nominal story line, this one had none. The partygoers were thrust straight into the action on the bed, where a young girl was grappling with a boy. His face was consistently turned away from the camera; on hers, expression ran the gamut from acquiescence, to protest, to terror, as the boy first fondled her, then tied her to the bedposts and, finally, held a gun to her head. The girl screamed; the boy pulled the trigger; the screen went blank.

The young man who had brought the film in squirmed as he looked at the two police officers with whom he had just viewed it for the second time.

"You see what I mean?" he said. "It looks so real. I mean, maybe she's an actress, maybe it was all a joke, but . . . it just looks so real."

The police officers agreed. To them, it looked like murder.

They tried to match the girl on the screen to descriptions of girls reported missing, with no result. No unclaimed bodies in the morgue resembled her. The girl looked about fifteen years old. The police canvassed area schools and youth hangouts until they stumbled on the right one and someone said, "That's Julie. She lives over on the Heights."

Two officers went to Julie's home, prepared to break a parent's heart. When they knocked at the door, it was Julie who answered.

At first, she denied all knowledge of the video.

The police were adamant.

Under pressure from them and from her parents, Julie changed her story. Reading it made me feel very old.

The social pyramid at Julie's school was dominated by a dozen of Kingsport's more privileged youth, who had banded together to form a club they called The King's Sports. The sport they pursued was sex for points, with points awarded according to the degree of difficulty in persuading a given target to cooperate, and the kind of sex ultimately performed. Proof had to be tangible, preferably in video format. Refusal to participate in the game made a girl a social pariah. Rumor and innuendo, harassment in the halls and swimming pool, had all been used to good effect more than once. At least one of Julie's classmates had been hounded from the school. Julie could not afford to follow. So she gave in, to what she thought at first would be straight sex with a guy who, though she didn't like him, was "at least not a total geek. Kids are going to do it anyway," she was quoted as saying, "so what difference does it make who it's with?"

Her words were desperately nonchalant. I found them appalling, not least because I suspected she believed them.

Julie had protested the video recording, been frightened at being tied up, and had panicked absolutely at the appearance of the gun. "But it wasn't real, so it's no big deal, right?"

She refused to press charges, and the story died.

Two weeks later, the Youth Development Project had been officially called into being. Its lofty purpose was to "impart to the youth of our city a sense of civic commitment and moral responsibility through community service works." Initial funding for this noble enterprise had come from none other than John Randall Outray II, father of Randy and Simone.

A week or so later an edict had come down from the Board of Education, outlawing the formation of private clubs or secret societies within the schools. Any student caught violating this order faced automatic expulsion.

I needed a coffee. Actually, I needed a drink, but the bars weren't open yet and I didn't feel like going all the way home. A glance around the half-empty room persuaded me I wasn't in any danger of being desk-less when I returned, so I decided to go to the coffee shop next door for a break. Stretching the kinks out of my neck, I rose and gathered my printouts together and put them in my bag.

Coffee with Cream did most of its business in take-out but for those who preferred to linger, there was a scatter of tables and chairs. Early morning was my favorite time to stop by, when the cranberry muffins were still hot out of the oven and the bustling activity of people on their way to work lent the illusion I belonged to a bigger whole. This would be my second visit of the day.

It was just past eleven when I went in. Jana looked up in surprise from the beans she was grinding.

"Well, hi. Again. Do you need another muffin fix?"

"Just coffee. I'm a one-muffin-a-day girl. Let me try some of that new blend, what do you call it? Mocha Java Jive. It sounds too racy for first thing in the morning, but I think I can handle it now."

I took my coffee to a seat by the window. A handful of women had commandeered three of the tables around it. Judging by the casual clothes they were wearing and the fatigue lining some of their faces, I guessed they were the stay-at-home moms of young children. The kids were probably at Storytime next door or the play school down the block. The very ordinariness of it all made the story I had just read seem that much more surreal. I wondered how these mothers would react if, ten or twelve years hence, their children made snuff films for kicks. Their chatter skated over cartoons, preschool programs, and street-proofing. The voice of a frail brunette who looked far too young to be anybody's mother, rose above the rest.

"Well, I can tell you right now, if anyone ever so much as touched Dustin, I'd kill him."

"An eye for an eye?" someone said, trying for levity. "Tsk. Tsk. That's politically incorrect, you know."

"Don't you believe it. Vengeance is what the judicial system is all about. It's just that now, instead of going out and evening up the score yourself, there's some nice, impersonal machinery in place to get your eye for you."

"Retribution without personal guilt."

"Why not, they've got guilt-free everything else these days. Speaking of which, have you tried those new guiltless potato chips?"

"Tried them? I ate a whole bag yesterday afternoon. Don't talk to me about guilt-free." And the conversation slipped easily back into things that really matter.

I left Coffee with Cream a few minutes later.

My study carrel had been taken over by a girl in a short black skirt and a pair of thick-soled shoes that made her legs look as skinny as Olive Oyl's. I had noticed her earlier, sitting on the other side of the room, and I supposed she had moved to take advantage of the natural light from the window. I retreated to the spot she had vacated and went back to work.

My second lead was more difficult to trace. I wanted to know what had prompted Randy's withdrawal from college. The fact that whatever it was had resulted in a donation large enough, according to Sonja, to finance a new library, meant it had to be serious enough for some fairly elaborate camouflage. Granite College would have wanted its good name protected as much as the Outrays did theirs.

The story would not have appeared in the *Barker*. Not only did Granite lie outside its natural sphere, the *Barker's* loyalty to the Outrays had always been unquestioned. But I couldn't believe the *Express* would have passed it up. Its publisher, Milo Rajacic, had a workingman's disdain for the moneyed upper class, and his reporters were specially trained to sniff out tidbits to discredit them. His scope was statewide, his nose unerring.

New Hampshire roughly resembles a right triangle, with its longest side running north to south. Rolling foothills slope down to the Atlantic Ocean on the southeast, while the north is cut by the several ranges of the White Mountains. For the most part, the granite for which the state is nicknamed resisted the advance of the glaciers. Where the ice did manage to cut through, it left a series of ruggedly scenic notches, in one of which Hawthorne's *Old Man in the Mountain* scowls. In another, lies the town of Wells, where Granite College was established in 1905. It is a private school, attended by the sons and daughters of the wealthy, who began flocking to the area when the lavish Mt. Washington Hotel opened at the turn of the century. Nearby Bretton Woods enjoyed its resort-town heyday in the pre-depression years, when as many as fifty trains arrived every day and private railroad cars sat on a siding by the golf course, waiting to take their passengers home. It seemed a fitting place for the 1944 meeting of the World Monetary Fund, at which they set the gold standard at thirty-five dollars an ounce, and established the American dollar as the cornerstone of international financial exchange.

Ten miles down the road, the College reflected this stellar past.

I opened an Internet search on the Outrays and found nothing remotely incriminating, then tried the College, with the same result. What about the town of Wells itself? I tapped the name into the computer and was rewarded with a dozen listings. I pulled all of them and read them through, discarding most as irrelevant. Three held my attention.

The byline on all of these belonged to a *Daily Express* reporter well known for her dogged pursuit of a story. In this case, she had tried her best on three separate occasions to stir up controversy, but no one had been buying and the story finally died. Once again, it centered on sex and videos.

The basic premise was the same as that in the high school efforts, but the product was aesthetically superior and the age of the female participants considerably advanced. These were not schoolgirls, motivated by curiosity or fear of rejection. These were affluent, bored housewives, attracted by the youth and vigor of the college boys and more than willing to participate in an afternoon of uninhibited, and they hoped anonymous, sex. Their shock at finding *Afternoon Encounters* for sale was total.

This was the ripple that had alerted the prescient *Express* reporter. Unfortunately, she didn't move fast enough. The wives in question presented a solid wall of "no comment" beyond which she could not penetrate. Though she managed somehow to obtain a copy of *Afternoon Encounters*, and even to identify one of the women, the male lead had been careful never to show his face to the camera. His partner flatly refused to name him. Curious, I searched the files for any other reference to her, and found a brief social note describing her plans for an extended trip abroad.

I went back to the list of stories about the College and found several references to the generous donation that was making the new library possible. Randy Outray was not mentioned, but the timing was right. I was convinced he had masterminded *Afternoon Encounters*.

I left the library just as they were closing. I wasn't sure that what I'd learned put me any farther ahead. I had proof, if any was needed, that Randy Outray was seriously disturbed. I had confirmed, for what it was worth, that when the chips were down, his family would drop buckets of money on the table to clean up the mess. But I had already known that Randy was arrogant and willful and without conscience. What I still didn't know was who had killed him, or why.

It seemed unlikely that any of the people involved with the King's Sports or Granite College scandals had done it. The size of the payoffs would have diffused any lingering resentments, and the girls and women involved seemed to have been willing participants in the games and reluctant to lay any blame at all on Randy Outray.

CHAPTER TWENTY-SIX

Brent William's apartment had undergone some major changes since my first visit. The ratty couch was gone, to be replaced by a sofa and chairs covered in some nubby material and flanked by low wooden tables. The computer system I had last seen perched on a box was now housed in a vast corner unit that combined bookshelves with workspace and left room for a printer. Area rugs in bold Indian print marked the room's separate functions. Only the leafy green plant was still the same, though the gift card had at last been removed.

Brent shyly introduced me to the author of these changes.

"This is Rolph," he said, and I got a bone-melting smile from a six-foot hunk dressed in form-fitting jeans, a sweatshirt, and an apron.

"I'm a chef," he explained, dusting off a floury hand before shaking mine. "It's my day off. I'm experimenting with some almond pastry in the kitchen." He winked. "Sometimes it pays to make the mistakes at home, before taking the show on the road."

"Whatever it is smells terrific," I said, slipping out of my boots.

"If it works, you can test it later." Rolph flashed me the smile again and disappeared back into the kitchen. It was probably the worst kind of sexism but I couldn't repress the thought: what a waste.

Brent had things organized for us in the living room. He had drawn up a side chair for me at the desk. Paper and sharpened pencils were out. The computer was on.

"We're all set," he said. "Where do you want to go?"

I felt like a fraud. I had invited myself over on the pretext of wanting a first-hand demonstration of the kind of service he planned to offer his clients. I had brought his prospectus and my notes on it with me, and I fully intended to review them with him. But first I wanted to steer our course toward the seamier side of Kingsport life.

I said, "What can you tell me about The Clubbe?"

Brent shot me a look.

"The Kingsport Clubbe," I said.

It was the only lead I had left. What had started as the kind of brandy and cigars club acceptable to the Protestant social ethic of its day, had lost something of its rarefied air over the years. Though preservation of the old-boy network was still a key factor, physical fitness now had the edge over purely social encounter. That some of the fitness instructors and massage therapists might offer services beyond those outlined in the Clubbe's brochure, was tacitly understood. No doubt the wives objected, and judging by the rather desperate measures some of them adopted in remodeling themselves in a more nubile image, some of them at least felt seriously threatened.

Given what I had learned that morning about Randy Outray's entrepreneurial assays, The Clubbe seemed an appropriate next stop.

Brent's face was tight as he chased information across the computer screen. "Why do you want this stuff?" he asked suddenly. I glanced up sharply. He was blushing. It was on the tip of my tongue to ask why, when it hit me.

Brent already knew about The Clubbe. And since he would hardly qualify for membership on the basis of social standing, he must have been an employee. Clearly, it was a source of embarrassment. Equally clearly, he thought *he* was the reason for my questions.

I said, "I'm sorry, Brent, I didn't realize you . . . "

"No?" he said nastily. His voice was pitched higher than normal. "Then why are you asking about it? Are personal background checks a normal part of your business assessment service?"

Sensing trouble, Rolph had left the kitchen and come to stand behind Brent's chair, his presence lending reassurance. "What's going on?"

Two bright spots of anger burned in Brent's pale cheeks. He looked very young.

I said again, quickly, "I'm sorry. I had no idea you'd ever worked at The Clubbe, Brent, honestly. That's not why I was asking."

I eyed them both hesitantly, then plunged. "Look. I'm trying to find out anything I can about Randy Outray that might explain why someone would kill him. The Clubbe is the only lead I have."

If I expected astonishment, I was disappointed. After a brief silence, Rolph said only, "I thought the police suspected that guy, Forrester, the one whose wife and little girl were murdered. And his brother, what's his name? Maitland."

Brent looked startled. "Maitland? Wasn't he . . . ?"

"Yes," I said quickly. "He was. But they didn't do it, either of them."

Rolph smiled at my vehemence and I saw his hand tighten on Brent's shoulder. He tilted his head in the direction of the living area. "Maybe we'd be more comfortable over there."

I chose one of the nubby chairs, curling into it with my feet tucked underneath me. Rolph and Brent sat side by side on the couch. They weren't touching, but the connection between them was palpable.

I cleared my throat while I thought about where to begin.

Brent recovered his poise faster than I did. "Why don't you tell us what drew your attention to The Clubbe in the first place," he suggested, "And we'll go on from there."

"Okay," I said, "Here goes. You know what I do for a living, apart from the course at Metcalf?"

Brent nodded.

"Well, because of the role I play in their lives, some of my clients talk to me, probably more than they should, about things that are going on in Kingsport and who is doing what to whom. You know the kind of thing I mean."

Brent nodded again.

"Since Susan and Tracey Forrester were murdered, the Outrays, and Randy in particular, have come in for their more than their fair share of speculation and gossip. So this morning I thought I'd take a look at the news clipping service at the library and see if I could follow up on some of it."

At this point in my recitation, Rolph got up and left the room. I heard water running in the kitchen, then the soft clink of china as he assembled a tea tray. I hoped he'd put some food out with it. The cranberry muffins seemed a long time ago.

"And could you?" said Brent.

"Yes. I found two quite recent incidents involving Randy Outray. Unfortunately, although he was the bad guy in both of them, the victims, if you'd call them that, refused to press charges and may even have benefited. Financially, I mean. The only solid thing I have to go on is that both incidents involved sex and videotapes. And I thought that since Randy, along with almost every other guy in town with half a million or more in the bank, is a member of The Clubbe, that that would make a good next step."

Rolph came in with the tea things. I stopped talking and accepted some lemon tea, though I would have preferred a mug to the delicate china cup he handed me. I was always afraid I'm going to break off the little handles. As a chef, I gathered Rolph subscribed to the theory that tea always tastes better drunk out of porcelain.

He lifted a plate of pastries. "Willing to test my experiment?"

I imagined my body ballooning from indulgence, like rising dough, as I selected what looked like a miniature turnover from the plate and bit into it. Raspberry jam gushed over my chin. Rolph dashed to my rescue with a napkin.

"I'll have to make those smaller," he said with a grin, "So you can eat them in a single bite."

I laughed. "They are a little messy. But definitely worth it," I added, as I popped the second half into my mouth.

A few minutes passed in silence as the three of us munched and sipped. Then Brent said, "So what is it you want to find out about The Clubbe? You know who the members are. I'm sure you have a pretty good idea of what goes on there. How does that help?"

I set my empty teacup back on the table and shook my head at Rolph's offer of more. "I don't know," I said. "I'm not sure exactly what I thought I could uncover. Some incident that could lead to murder, I guess. A grudge? More videos?" I shrugged, palms up. "I don't know. I suppose I hoped the Internet could produce a miracle for me."

Brent shook his head. "If you could sneak in the back door, it might tell you who owes money, who pays extra for extra services. But I think what you're looking for is the kind of thing no one in their right mind would ever commit to a computer."

Rolph snorted. "Are you kidding me? You could probably find naked pictures of your grandma on the net if you looked hard enough. People put anything and everything out there. There's no such thing as privacy any more. Or personal dignity, either. It's blackmail heaven."

Brent and I gaped at each other like goldfish.

The silence in the room was absolute.

"Well," I finally managed. "There's a thought. More than one blackmail victim has turned on his abuser before now. It would certainly give us a motive. But what sort of hold could Randy have had on anyone? It's not as though what goes on at The Clubbe is exactly a secret, or even particularly blackmail-worthy, come to that. Not these days."

"You'd be surprised," Rolph said, "at what some people get up to. No pun intended."

"Whips and chains?" I made a moue of distaste.

Rolph waved an airy hand. "That's old hat. Actually, I was thinking more along the lines of erotic asphyxiation. You know— gaspers. That kind of thing can get out of hand pretty easily."

I stared.

Rolph patted my knee. "Don't worry. Most of the folks you know have fairly pedestrian tastes. Just not ones they like to advertise. What d'you think Brent was doing there? Does he look like a security guard to you?"

I bit my lip.

Brent interpreted my silence as disapproval. "You probably

think it's disgusting. My mother certainly did, but the money was good, and I already knew I was gay. So why not?"

His words were almost an echo of the girl Julie's, of snuff film fame, and I felt the same sense of despair I had felt over her. How could a young man like Brent value himself so little?

Into the pause, Rolph said, "Then, there a few club members with a strong preference for the very young."

Brent said, "That's when I left, when I found that out. I hadn't actually been working there very long and one night I saw this girl, maybe fifteen years old, waiting in the lounge. She was dressed in this short little pleated skirt and knee socks and I thought she was somebody's kid, you know, in her school uniform or something. She told me she had a date with one of the 'gentlemen'."

I felt my gorge rise. Sex, even kinky sex, between consenting adults is one thing; this was something else. It took me a minute to ask, "Who was the 'gentleman,' do you know?"

Brent shook his head. "I never saw him. I never saw her again, either. But I left there just a few days later anyway, so that's not surprising."

I sighed. Anything else was too much to hope for, I supposed.

Rolph said, "I heard a few rumors."

"You? Did you work there too?"

"Oh, no, I didn't work there. I was a member."

I made a conscious effort not to let my jaw drop.

"They asked me to leave when I overstepped the bounds of propriety and told everyone right out loud that I was gay." His tone was self-mocking. "Not only gay, but a cook. Imagine the shame for my poor papa. Lucky for me, the Lynden millions were all neatly tied up in trusts or I would have been cut off without the proverbial cent."

"You're Rolph *Lynden*?"

"The skeleton in the closet, himself." He grinned. "Only I came out."

I remembered the uproar. It was all Sonja Reid had talked about for weeks.

"But I don't get it. From what you guys have said, I gather that some of the other Clubbe members are, if not gay, then at least bisexual. So why kick you out?"

"Tsk, tsk. You're showing your class. The upper strata always preserve appearances. In fact, in our rarified circles, appearance matters more than reality."

"I see," I said. "It's one thing to be different and something else to acknowledge it. No wonder psychiatrists do such good business."

Brent was stacking the dirty cups back on the tray. I liked the way these two divvied up the household chores like an old married couple. I wondered how long they had been together.

Brent said, "So which ones did go for the kids?"

"It's only rumor," Rolph cautioned.

I understood his hesitation. This was not a finger to point casually.

"I did hear the girl was there for a date with a lawyer. This was a really smart guy, with a great sense of humor—very popular with the ladies, and I never had the least suspicion before that there was anything wrong with him. Anyway, I'm sure you've heard of him. It was Mel Deloitte."

I felt the color drain from my face.

I scarcely heard the details of what Rolph said after that, something about Deloitte's marriage and how bitter the divorce had been.

Mel Deloitte? It wasn't possible. He was Kingsport's most eligible man, women panted after him. Why would he hit on little girls? My stomach roiled at the thought. Hard behind it, came the realization that it was almost too perfect a scenario. Who better for Randy to put the screws to than a family friend whose career would be toast if his special interest came to light? The ladies of Kingsport, and the police, might turn a blind eye to most of what went on at The Clubbe, but there was no way they would ignore this. I had a sudden, vivid recollection of Simone Outray's bitter statement at the Reid's party. "I know what kind of 'working out' they do there. They think I don't, but I do." I wondered if someone had told her about the children. And who more likely to have done it than her brother?

If it was true, Randy Outray must have been a fool to put himself so completely in the hands of his blackmail victim. On the other hand, what choice had he had? Mel Deloitte had been the Outray's lawyer for twenty-five years. How could Randy possibly explain wanting someone else to represent him, without exposing his criminal sideline to his parents? Rolph had been right about that. In those circles, you could do anything you wanted, as long as you didn't get caught. Maybe an end to the blackmail was to be Mel's payment for getting Randy off on the murder charge.

Another question nagged like a persistent fly that wouldn't be swatted. How much did Kerrin know of this?

I became aware of Brent, hovering anxiously by my chair. "Are you all right, Nina? Do you want a glass of water or a drink or something?"

I grabbed at the fraying edges of my composure.

"Tell me something, Brent. Did you know Mel Deloitte at The Clubbe at all? Is that how you came to be on the mock jury?"

"No," said Brent. "I never met him. It was Kerrin Adams who asked me to be on the jury. A friend of a friend recommended me when she was installing her new computer and I customized some software for her. She asked if I'd be interested in working on a trial run of a case sometime and I said sure. When she called me up, I didn't know it was going to be the Outray case, or I probably would have backed out. I didn't know the guy personally, but I knew of him, you know what I mean?"

I didn't question my willing suspension of disbelief at the flimsy evidence of Mel Deloitte's guilt. Anything, it seemed, no matter how bizarre, that pointed the finger of accusation away from David, was fair game.

By now, Brent and Rolph had fully entered into the spirit of the thing.

"What about a weapon?" Brent was asking. "We have a victim,

and we have a motive. We still need the other two, what are they, opportunity and means. Does Deloitte own a gun? What was Randy shot with, anyway, a .22?"

"You watch too much television," Rolph said fondly. "I had the radio on in the kitchen and according to the latest news report, it was a derringer."

"Isn't that kind of an old-fashioned gun?" Brent asked.

"Yeah, I don't know if they're made any more, but there are some around, family heirloom type things. I think it was a derringer that Booth used to shoot Lincoln."

Still with the feeling of watching actors on a stage, I saw Brent get up and go over to the computer. "It's pretty convenient, having a computerized encyclopedia," he said, as the printer whirred. A minute later, he handed me two sheets of paper. One gave me the history of the derringer pistol. The other showed me what it looked like.

What it looked like was a toy. Small enough to fit easily into a pocket, it held only two shots. One had been used on Randy Outray. I wondered if Mel had plans for the other one.

I stared at the picture numbly.

Rolph said, "Have you ever seen a gun at Deloitte's house, Nina? He doesn't keep a little pistol like that," he pointed to the paper in my hand, "In his desk drawer by any chance?"

"He doesn't need to," I said, my voice sounding hollow. "The walls of his study are practically papered with the damn things. He's a collector."

CHAPTER TWENTY-SEVEN

My first impulse was to call in the police right then and there. Some fleeting rag of sensibility eventually persuaded me that I had to be sure of his guilt, beyond all reasonable doubt, before I destroyed a man's life.

When I considered it rationally, all I really had to go on was hearsay and circumstance. Rumor might say anything about anyone; Rolph had no eyewitness evidence that Mel Deloitte favored children; indeed, he and Brent only knew of the single episode of a young girl coming to The Clubbe, which made blackmail no more than a flimsy theory. As to the weapon involved, lots of people owned guns, even derringers. But that, at least, gave me a place to start.

It was quite true that the walls of Deloitte's study were laden with firearms, but I had no idea if there was a derringer among them. I tended to notice only the larger items in his collection, the Winchesters and the Remingtons, whose polished stocks made them look more like works of art than instruments of death. Until now, the smaller pistols had held no real interest for me.

A key to Deloitte's house was locked in my father's old bureau at home, along with other keys entrusted to me by clients who naturally anticipated that I would use them only to do my job, not to spy on them, or to search their homes for evidence of guilt in a murder. As I slipped Deloitte's key into my pocket, I suffered a pang of conscience in which I clearly heard my mother's voice telling me to respect other people's privacy. For an instant, I wavered.

Such are our defining moments: we do something, or refrain from doing it, and so create the pattern of our lives.

I debated having something to eat before going back out, but decided not to take the time. Instead, I stuffed a chocolate bar into my pocket as a buffer against the fatigue that was beginning to drag at me.

When I used my key to open Mel Deloitte's back door, it was just after six o'clock. The house was quiet. As a matter of course, I'd rung the doorbell first, but I knew Mel had a regular dinner meeting of the local bar association on Wednesday nights and it wasn't likely he'd be home much before ten. I wasn't worried about the neighbors; houses in that part of town were set far enough apart to ensure privacy.

Deloitte had timers on several lights, including the one in the kitchen, because he hated coming in to a dark house. Down the hall, the study was deeply shadowed, but as it didn't face the street, it was unlikely anyone would notice if I turned on a lamp.

It was a high room, with two velvet-draped windows overlooking the ravine. At one end, it opened to a second floor accessible by a spiral stair. On the outside, this part of the house looked like the turret of a castle. Inside, it reminded me of Professor Higgins' library. Now I wondered if Mel Deloitte had brought any Eliza Dolittles here for instruction.

The second floor was warmed and darkened by oak bookshelves that lined the walls from floor to ceiling. On the main floor, the shelves stopped at mid-point. The upper half of the wall was covered in grasscloth, against which Deloitte's gun collection was displayed.

At a glance I could see nothing missing, no telltale lighter patches against the wallpaper, where something might have been removed. When I considered it, there was no reason why there should be. If Mel had used one of his own guns to shoot Randy Outray, he could simply have brought it home again and hung it back where it belonged.

I made a careful tour of the room, comparing the smaller firearms on the walls with the picture of the derringer that Brent had printed for me. Eventually, I found a pair of them by the door, hung at an angle to each other, so that they framed a blurred daguerreotype underneath.

I squinted at the woman in the picture. She was dressed with the fussy elegance of the late nineteenth century, her expression severe. There was something vaguely familiar in the set of her mouth and the shape of her nose that made me wonder if she were one of Mel's ancestors and if the pistols had once belonged to her.

With no clear idea of what I was doing, I lifted the little guns from the wall one at a time, and looked them over. On police shows, the experts seem to be able to tell if a gun has been recently fired by sniffing the barrel. Holding each in turn gingerly, afraid one or the other might go off accidentally in my hands, I inhaled cautiously in the direction of the barrel.

All I noticed was a mild, greasy smell.

I didn't know how to tell if the guns were loaded, and wasn't sure I wanted to find out.

I'd been a fool to come. What had I really hoped to accomplish on my own? I was Debbie Domestic, not Dick Tracy. As I hung the derringers carefully back on the wall, I noticed that my hands were shaking.

Then I heard him.

At first, I thought it was the surge of my own racing pulses that nailed me to the doorjamb. Then I realized it was the muffled thunk of the heavy front door closing.

I glanced at my watch. It was barely six-thirty. The meeting must have been canceled, or maybe Deloitte had decided not to stay to dinner. Whatever the reason, I didn't want him to find me here in his study with his guns. I was across the room and up the narrow, winding stairs to the shadows in the loft before I finished the thought.

It didn't occur to me then that I could simply have stayed where I was and told Mel I'd been doing some work on his ledgers. There was no reason for him not to believe me, no reason for him to suspect I suspected him of murder, nothing except my own fear and guilt at trespassing in someone else's home.

Apart from a leather easy chair and an antique Spanish chest, the loft was empty of furniture, and by extension, hiding places. Luckily, the lamp I had turned on downstairs was shaded to fall on the desk. The loft was nearly dark.

I eyed the chest, which was deep but not very long. The bulk of the padded jacket I was wearing only added to the problem of space, but I managed to wedge myself between the chest and the shelves behind it, hoping that, from below, I would be invisible.

Deloitte entered the study and went straight to his desk. That the light was on didn't seem to register with him, or maybe he assumed the timer on it had clicked over. I heard him curse mildly as he shuffled files, opening and closing the drawers in the cabinet where he kept some of his correspondence. My heart thudded. He'd forgotten something he needed for the meeting; that was all. He had only come back to pick it up. Just a few minutes, I told myself, a few minutes, and he'll be gone.

There was silence now below me. Willing myself not to poke my head up over the top of the chest to look, I decided Mel must be reading something over, determining that the file in his hand was in fact the one he wanted.

The muscles in my right leg started to spasm. I held my breath and moved fractionally to relieve the pain. As I shifted my weight, my boot scraped against the side of the chest. It was the smallest of sounds, but it filled the silence in the room like thunder.

Paper rustled as Mel dropped the file he was holding back onto the desk. I heard another drawer slide open, and then he started for the stairs.

My stomach muscles clenched.

From my pathetic hiding place I could not see him, but I heard the climbing steps and knew where he was when he stopped, his head only a few feet below the level of the top stair. I could hear him breathing. He was looking up, but I didn't think he could see me at that angle. I didn't move. In any event, it was too late now for escape. I remembered the walls full of guns in the study below and stayed where I was, crouched, not breathing, against the Spanish chest.

Deloitte paused where he was for a few seconds, then I heard him climbing back down the stairs. For one foolish moment I thought maybe he was satisfied, that he would collect the forgotten file from his desk and leave the house.

He stood very still in the room below me, waiting.

From my dubious shelter, I felt as if some sort of mental censor had suddenly dropped into place, separating me from reality. I was invisible, inaudible, powerless, the dreamer of the dream.

I suppose nobody ever believes that they will really die. I'm sure Susan Forrester felt this same strange sense of unreality as she watched her murderer raise his knife. I'm sure she thought, as I did, that something would happen to stop him. Other people might be murdered, but not me.

I felt a sharp twist of pain in my cheek, where it was pressed against one of the brass hinges of the trunk. Touching my fingers to it, I found my face was wet with tears.

I once read somewhere that when a man is hunted for his life, one of the greatest dangers he faces is the overpowering urge to give himself up. I hadn't believed it. I had always thought that fear would drive him until he dropped, like a hunted rabbit. But I found out that it's true. Whether it was fear, or fatigue, or the blind instinct of the hunted, the impulse to surrender came and I didn't even try to resist it.

I stood up, wiped my tear-stained cheeks with my hands, and started shakily down the stairs.

As I got to ground level, I stumbled and nearly fell. Deloitte took hold of my arm from behind; I felt my skin shrink from his touch. He spun me around and I saw his eyes widen as the light fell on my face.

"Nina? My God, what are you doing here? You scared me half to death. Jesus, I thought you were a burglar or something. I might have killed you!"

There was genuine horror in his voice. For the first time, I noticed that there was a gun in his right hand, not a derringer, but something larger and heavier that looked infinitely more deadly. The hand that held it was shaking almost as badly as mine had done.

"My God," Mel said again. "I had no idea you were here. I didn't see your car outside. I just ran in to pick up a file and I heard . . . I could see . . . that there was someone there and I took the gun out of my drawer and . . . Jesus, why didn't you say anything?"

I almost wept with relief. Mel Deloitte wasn't going to shoot me. My bullet-ridden body wasn't going to tumble grotesquely down the twisting stairs onto the Aubusson carpet below. I sent a brief prayer of thanks heavenward.

As he spoke, Deloitte had laid the gun carefully back in the drawer, shutting it with a decisive click. When I realized he was still staring at me, waiting for me to explain why I had been hiding behind the chest in his study loft, I took the lead he had given me, crossing my fingers on the lie the way Kerrin and I had when we were kids.

"I just stopped in to check on a couple of things. I thought you'd be at your dinner meeting so I wouldn't be disturbing you, but just as I was leaving, I heard someone in the hall. I guess I've been a little jumpy the last few days and, like you, my first reaction was 'burglar!' If I'd known it was you . . . "

I let my voice trail off in a suitably shaken tremolo.

For the second time in as many days, I watched Mel Deloitte down a snifter of brandy in a single gulp. This time though, he offered me one as well. It produced the same effect as the brandy I had drunk at Ian Forrester's, but it tasted a whole lot better. We spent about five minutes assuring one another that no harm had been done.

"Where is your car anyway?" Mel finally said. "It's not in the drive."

"I parked it where I always do, on the far side of the garage. If you came up by the front door, you wouldn't have seen it."

Mel's glass went down with a bang. "Christ, I forgot I left the engine running." He checked his watch and scooped up a file folder. "Look, if you're done here—you're sure you're all right?—how about I see you out. I'm low on gas as it is and I have to get back to that meeting."

At the door to the study, he stopped and tucked the folder under his arm, freeing his hands to straighten one of the derringers on the wall. I felt my mouth go dry.

"These things are always shifting," he complained.

"Who's the woman in the picture?" I said, trying to keep my voice even. "Your grandmother?"

"Great-grandmother," Mel corrected. "On my father's side. Derringers were considered acceptable ladies' weapons in her day, and I gather she liked to feel well-protected, though God knows she looks as if she could have repelled any boarders by force of personality alone. As far as I know, neither of these little guns has ever been fired."

CHAPTER TWENTY-EIGHT

It must have been nearly three when something woke me. For some time, I lay in that heavy state mid-way between sleep and waking, where it is hard to separate reality from dream. Something had woken me, but whether I had heard a noise, or whether it was the dream itself that had startled me awake, I couldn't tell. I puffed the pillow under my head and prepared to drift back to sleep again.

Thirty minutes later, I gave it up and decided I might as well brew a pot of tea and pick up where I'd left off in the latest issue of *Traveler* magazine.

As I crossed the living room to the wicker basket where I keep my magazines, some movement outside caught my eye, and I went to the window for a closer look. Light from the streetlamp filtered through the shutters and the Boston fern that screened the glass. The movement I had seen was simply a shadow falling across the light, as some other wakeful soul walked his dog in the pre-dawn quiet. Perhaps it was their outbound journey that had woken me. A few delicate flakes of snow were falling, and I found myself envying the stranger and his dog strolling so peacefully through them. I often attribute to other people a state of mind lacking in myself. For all I know, the man on the street was no more at peace than I was, but it comforted me to imagine him so.

My own feelings remained nearly as jumbled as when I had first arrived home after my little escapade at Mel Deloitte's.

I still tasted gall when I thought about it. How could I have been so stupid? I had been willing enough to assume Mel Deloitte's guilt to breach his trust. I had broken into his home looking for evidence to implicate him in a murder, then lied to him about my reasons for being there. Why? How could it have been so easy for me to believe such things about a man I knew and respected?

The whip flicked me again. Not only my face, my whole body burned. I had wanted Deloitte to be the answer. Or at least, I had wanted David not to be. Every bone and fiber of my being rebelled at the thought that I might still have been wrong about David, but I no longer believed that Mel Deloitte had had anything to do with the murder of Randy Outray. His horrified distress at nearly shooting me had convinced me of that. Whether he was guilty of the other thing, I didn't know, but considering it now, rationally, I didn't think so. Based on my own knowledge of the man, it just didn't seem credible. Whatever gossip Rolph had heard, had probably been just that; gossip. After seeing the damage innuendo and rumor had done to Ian Forrester, I was appalled at how nearly I had set someone else in the same trap.

In the kitchen, the kettle started whistling. I abandoned the window and the now-empty street, and went to make my tea. Someone had given me a selection of herbal teas as a gift a few months ago and though I normally drank orange pekoe, tonight I chose chamomile, hoping it would help me sleep.

I curled into the window seat, magazine open but unread, and thought about David. He had left a brief message on my machine that I hadn't noticed when I stopped to pick up Deloitte's key. He had called to let me know he was taking Ian to a nursing home in Concord, away from the publicity, and the police, in Kingsport. He would stay overnight with his parents and return in the morning.

I wondered if the watcher in the green car would follow him all the way to Concord and back.

I could understand him wanting to get Ian out of the public eye. Things had been bad enough before, but now, with David a suspect in Randy Outray's murder, they would be intolerable. I thought too, that with Ian safely tucked into a nursing home, David would have a freer hand to look after himself.

I bit my lip.

That was the crux of it.

I had seen David as a chance to make amends for all the times I had failed to look after the people I loved. All the desperate wanting, the good intentions, the heartache had not saved Brian or Rory or my mother or even, finally, Kerrin. What had happened to each of them had been something totally out of my control. They had been lost beyond my power to save them.

This time there was no creeping disease, no devastating accident, no death of hope. This time, it wasn't fate that mattered, but facts, and I had wanted to be the one to present them. But it seemed that that, too, was beyond my power.

The grandfather clock chimed five. Looking up at it, I realized with a kind of shock that I still considered that clock to be my father's. So much of what I lived with seemed still to belong to someone else. My mother's table, my father's clock, Brian's wine glasses. Only my guilt was my own.

Maybe it was time to let it go.

I rinsed the empty teapot and set it on the stove. Sleepy Time had not fulfilled its promise; the sandman had apparently gone for good.

Outside, the snow had stopped falling. The stars were fading. I slipped into jeans and my padded jacket and, wrapping a scarf around my neck, went out.

*

The path through the cemetery was dusted with snow. A single set of footprints had scuffed along it ahead of me, branching to the right where I held to the straight.

I had brought Christmas roses to lay on the graves of my family. I didn't, as a rule, bring tribute, but as I drove along Main Street in the gray dawn, supply trucks were just beginning to unload their wares at the grocer and the florist, ready for early Christmas rush opening. They nodded good morning as I slowed to a stop in front of Greavey's. It was exhilarating to be out and about at that time of day, when the street was quiet and the shops still waiting to be peopled. Mr. Greavey recognized me; if he thought it strange that I was buying flowers at five-thirty in the morning, he was kind enough not to say so.

Snow poofed under my feet when I opened the iron gate at St. John's, and it muffled my tread on the gravel path. To my left, the sliding sparkle of the river was crusted and mute. Even the air was still. An oak tree edged the path, ribbing it with shadows. Through its branches, I could see the morning star, shimmering blue-white, like frost. No ghosts stirred.

I laid the flowers gently in front of the polished black granite etched with my parents' names, then, with some hazy memory of a book I had read long ago, took two of the roses and scattered their pink petals over Rory's stone, and Brian's.

I waited for tears that did not come.

I breathed in the scent of the roses, sweet and heady, like a dream of summer nights. Closing my eyes, I could make out the familiar shapes of yesterday . . . my mother's smile, my father's hands, a baby's downy hair.

For the first time, I didn't flinch from memory. As I stood there in the pre-dawn stillness, I felt the past, so longed-after, so lived-over, slip off my shoulders like a burden.

*

The stars had guttered out by the time I headed back toward the gate. At the branch in the path I hesitated, half inclined to go home. But the events of the past few days still pressed on me, and the cemetery was quiet and solitary. I decided to walk on a little further, to the point where a hedge girdled monuments to the founders of Kingsport. Sprinkled like seeds around them were the graves of the lesser of their kin. It was where Randy Outray would be buried later that afternoon.

It gave me a queer feeling to be privy to so many of the secrets of his life, and his death. I had learned more about him than I wanted to know, and the old adage about familiarity breeding contempt had held true. I could summon no pity for him. Nor any regard.

Ahead of me gaped the oblong of Randy's grave. A black tarpaulin had been stretched protectively over it, making it look, from a distance, as though it were open. Behind it, euonymous bushes made a horizon against which the waning moon sketched a figure. The grounds man, I thought. And then I saw that it was not the grounds man at all. It was Simone Outray.

At my approach, she turned, as startled as if I were a ghost, her features blanched and dramatized in the milky light. Her figure was shrouded in what looked like an old army greatcoat, hands thrust deep into the pockets. Some violent emotion had drained her face to a mask.

I stopped short, embarrassed by her distress, and made awkward by my knowledge of her brother. We stared at each other across his grave.

"Hello, Simone," I said.

Her voice was a tentative half-whisper that carried no expression. "Miss Ryan?"

"Nina. Yes. I'm sorry, I didn't mean to intrude. I didn't realize anyone was here."

Simone said nothing. She looked dazed and witless, as if a touch would knock her over.

I drew a deep breath, forcing the conventional words. "Simone, I'm sorry about your brother. I know that's hardly an adequate thing to say, but what else is there? It's been a dreadful time for everyone."

A touch of something dark and clouded altered her face for a moment, something lost and uncertain moving like a stranger behind the mask. I had seen that look on her face before, in the hall at Reidmore.

"You didn't like him, did you, Nina?" she said.

"I didn't know him," I said helplessly.

"And now you never will. After all, he's dead."

It wasn't so much the casual phrasing that shocked me as the lack of something in her voice that ought to have been there. The effect was as startling and as definite as if she had sworn at me.

Her face frightened me. It still looked stupid, but I saw now that this was real; it was the blank stupidity of someone who is beyond feeling punishment, and who has long since stopped even asking the reason for it.

Memory stirred.

I was eight years old and Tommy Luna had cornered a stray dog in the lane behind our houses. Tommy had a stick and he kept poking it at the dog, forcing the animal further and further back into the corner between the fence and garbage cans. The dog was thin and straggly haired, with the same bruised look in his eyes that Simone had. Tommy was shouting and waving the stick around, pretending he was a lion tamer in the circus and we were the audience. The little dog cowered behind the garbage cans. Someone told Tommy to leave it alone and one of the little girls, maybe me, started crying, but Tommy wouldn't stop and when he poked out with the stick again, the little dog suddenly turned and jumped at him, sinking his teeth into Tommy's hand until Tommy screamed and dropped the stick. I thought the dog would run away then, but he didn't. He was still whimpering by the garbage cans when someone came with a muzzle and took him to the pound.

The memory spun away into silence, leaving me tingling with apprehension, wondering if I had really remembered it at all, or if it were just some trick of my imagination.

I stared at Simone Outray.

She didn't even need to speak. Her face told me all I wanted to know.

I suppose I should have felt relief that, after all, the police need not look any farther than Randy Outray's sister to find his murderer. But my stomach twisted with a sickening mix of pity, and the beginnings of fear. I remembered that the gun she had used to shoot her brother was small enough to fit inside a pocket, and the pockets of the coat she was wearing were wide and deep. "A derringer is a two-shot pistol" the encyclopedia had said. I wondered who Simone intended the second shot for.

Unreasoning panic stampeded my brain. The girl was in shock; I could hardly believe her capable of shooting anyone else, let alone me. Besides, I told myself, she had no reason to kill me, a virtual stranger, unless—and here I tasted blood as I bit my lower lip—unless she were insane. Fragments of what I had learned of her family whirled and resettled to form a different picture in my mind. I had been concentrating on Randy's history; I should have paid more attention to his sister's.

I grabbed at the fleeting rags of my common sense. Simone Outray wasn't crazy. That blank expression masked a working mind. She might choose to look retarded, but I sensed cunning behind the vacuous façade.

If I turned and ran now, would she follow me? I had no idea what the range of a derringer was.

Belatedly, I realized I had no idea whether she actually had a gun in her pocket at all.

"Simone," I began conversationally. My voice came out in a harsh croak. I cleared my throat and tried again, saying the first thing that came to mind. "Does your mother know you're here?"

"That bitch," she said. Her voice held no inflection. "She doesn't even know I'm alive." The calm voice broke. "I thought it would be different when Randy died. I thought she might turn to me, like mothers and daughters are supposed to, you know? Like, they tell you there's supposed to be this special bond, and all there really is, is this face, this perfect face, that ought to be smiling at you, staring at you like you just crawled out from under a rock or something." I could hear the tears behind her words. "Why couldn't she love me? She loved *him* and look how bad he messed up."

I bit my lip, unable to frame a response.

A feeble December sun was slowly brightening the sky. I wondered how long it would be before somebody showed up for work. Scanning the grounds, I saw no sign of any activity.

Simone moved and my head whipped around. Her right hand was fumbling in the pocket of her baggy coat, pulling out a little gun just like the ones I had seen hanging on the wall in Mel Deloitte's study. She held it vaguely pointed in my direction, looking down at it as though she were not quite sure where it had come from. The derringer looked like a toy in the hand of a child.

Oddly enough, now that I could see the gun, I wasn't frightened any more. It was as if fear had been raised to such a pitch that it had killed itself, like a light bulb flaring before it burns out. I faced the girl on the other side of Randy Outray's grave and said quite calmly, "Where did you get that?"

Simone looked at me then. Like her mother's, her eyes were very pale and clear. The dazed expression had vanished. She looked forlorn, and defenseless, and very, very young. She didn't answer my question directly.

"It's been in the family for a long time. Sort of an heirloom, I guess."

"Are you planning to shoot me with it?"

She looked astonished. "Why should I? You never did anything to me."

"What are you doing then? Trying to get even with your mother?"

She looked like such a child standing there in a coat several sizes too big, with a toy pistol in her hand. I thought of the time I had run away from home when I was six. My mother had scolded me for something and I remember thinking, I'll make her sorry. She'll miss me when I'm gone.

Simone watched me carefully. "You can't talk me out of it, you know," she said.

"No. I just thought I'd like to hear your side."

"Why? Nobody else has ever wanted to."

"What about Dr. Reeve? She's a good listener."

Simone shook her head. "I've been talking to Dr. Reeve since I was twelve years old. She's a nice lady. She still thinks she can help me. But she can't. It's too late."

I said impatiently, "Of course it isn't too late, Simone. You're just a kid. You can still turn things around."

"Not hardly. I shot him in the back. I can't even claim self-defense."

I found myself trying to make excuses for her. Only a few days ago, I had told David that I didn't believe murder was ever justified. In the context of what Randy Outray had done, that had been an easy position to take. Here, now, I wasn't so sure.

Simone wasn't looking for a trial; she had already passed her own judgment on her brother and on herself. I had been made an unwilling partner in the execution of her sentence, much as a real jury member might be, and I was learning that my instinct was to protect her life, rather than hurry it to its end.

"I'm sure the court could be made to understand," I said. "Your family has plenty of money. They can hire you a good lawyer."

She laughed harshly. "Yeah, right, the court. The court would have *excused* my brother Randy. Mel Deloitte would have fed them some bullshit story about how hard life had been to him, and he would have got off. That son of a bitch has never had to pay for anything in his life. I saw pictures of what he did to that woman and her little girl. Nothing can excuse that." Her eyes gleamed with tears. "Nothing can excuse me, either."

I felt defeated. I did not like Simone Outray, but I found I could not abandon her. "Let me help you," I said, wishing I meant it.

I saw her jaw tighten and her chin come up in a childish gesture of defiance. She shook her head again, hard, to dispel the tears. "There isn't any point. I hurt too much and I'm just so tired . . . don't you see, Nina? It'll be easier to be dead." She almost made it sound reasonable. "I'm sorry you came here. I meant to have it all over with before anybody was around. Hell, maybe they wouldn't even have noticed, just lowered Randy's coffin down right on top of my body."

Tears were streaming down my face. I made no move to brush them away.

Simone said, "Don't worry," in the gentle tone a mother might use to soothe a frightened child. "It's no big deal. Kids kill themselves all the time."

"That's ridiculous," I said. "You can't mean that."

For an answer, she raised the toy pistol to her head and pulled the trigger.

I was surprised how little sound it made.

CHAPTER TWENTY-NINE

The double funeral was on Christmas Eve in the afternoon. Sunshine glittered off fresh snow, and the cold, clear air brought color to exposed cheeks, making the knot of black-clad guests look more like carolers than mourners.

No one wept openly. The news of Simone's suicide and the revelation that it was she who had killed her brother, were shocks not yet fully absorbed. People took their cue from Zoe Outray, who stood rigidly at attention beside her husband. As gray-faced as his wife, John Outray watched the lowering caskets of his son and his daughter, touching a handkerchief to his lips with an unsteady hand. Neither of them acknowledged my presence. I couldn't blame them.

I had gone to their home sometime after the police informed them that their daughter had shot herself.

The housekeeper had let me in. Mrs. Palgrave was a tall, spare woman, with a face set in a permanent expression of disapproval. I waited as she took my coat and hung it away in a cupboard that seemed part of the molded paneling. Then I followed her down the hall.

I had never been inside the Outray mansion before; the hall seemed immense, mainly because it was very high and full of shadows cast by a chandelier like a frozen waterfall. The floor was a chilly chessboard of black and white marble that flowed to a series of closed doors.

Mrs. Palgrave showed me into a small room that I imagine was a sort of antechamber to the main living room. The furniture was French provincial, covered in rose silk. In one corner, a glass-fronted armoire displayed a collection of delicate ivory carvings that I recognized as netsuke. General Sanderson had a few of them and he took great pride in showing me the treasures he had acquired during his service in the Far East. Where his were lovingly tended, these had the look of museum pieces, valued for their monetary worth rather than their intrinsic beauty.

The room was cool enough for me to wish I had kept my jacket with me. There were logs laid in the fireplace. I doubted they were ever lit. From what I had seen, it was an elegant house, perfectly kept but the thought struck me forcibly that it was not, and had probably never been, a house for children.

The door behind me opened, and John and Zoe Outray came in.

Whatever I had thought of them before, I felt only pity for them now.

John shook my hand, murmuring "good of you to come." Zoe sank bonelessly into a chair and waited for whatever might happen next.

For the second time in just a few hours, I heard myself saying, "I'm sorry. I'm so very sorry for your loss. I wish there was something I could have done, something I could have said that might have prevented this from happening. But Simone was so upset . . . and so terribly determined."

I felt my throat starting to close and I stopped and swallowed, wishing violently for a glass of brandy.

Zoe sat very still, her calm demeanor a travesty of the poise I had witnessed at Sonja's party. Her pale eyes were fully open and she was crying soundlessly. John Outray stared at me with the concentration of a drunk trying to focus.

"Did she say anything at all before she . . . ?" he managed.

Their pain was palpable and I shrank from it. If I never told Simone's parents everything their daughter had said, I couldn't do it now. I swallowed again, and told them what I believed. "She loved you very much. And she hoped you would forgive her."

Zoe Outray gave an uncontrollable sob and folded in on herself in a desperate little gesture that broke something inside me. I went down on my knees in front of her chair. Her hands were covering her face. I took her wrists and gently pulled them down and held her hands in both my own.

"Don't, Mrs. Outray. Don't cry any more. You'll make yourself ill." I turned to her husband and said, "You should get her to bed. Tell Mrs. Palgrave to make her some tea and fill a hot water bottle. Her hands are like ice."

I turned back to Zoe Outray. She stared at me helplessly out of pale, drowned eyes. Her delicately made-up cheeks sagged slack and gray and her mouth was loose and blurred with crying. There was no beauty left; she looked old.

I heard the door open and John Outray murmur something to Mrs. Palgrave. Coming over to the chair, he touched his wife lightly on the shoulder and said, "Zoe? Can you get up? Let me help you, my dear."

She got to her feet slowly, stiffly, and her husband led her out into the hall. She went with him as obediently as if she were a sleepwalker.

At the foot of the stairs, John Outray turned to me and groped for unfamiliar words. "Thank you," he said.

The two of them disappeared upstairs. I let myself out.

*

David didn't attend the joint funeral that was held a few days later. Had it been Randy's alone, I wouldn't have gone either. But the time I'd spent with her had bonded me to Simone in ways I did not yet fully understand, and I needed to say goodbye.

Kerrin stood beside me through the graveside service. She had come to see me as soon as she heard what had happened. We talked long into the night, covering ground left untrodden for years, establishing a path for the future. And though I still mourned the loss of the old Kerrin and doubted we would ever meet for coffee on a regular basis, we seemed at least—at last—to have reached a peaceful plateau as siblings.

I looked over at Mel Deloitte, who stood at John Outray's shoulder as if to support him. Feeling my glance, he looked up and gave a brief nod. There was nothing to read in his face.

As the minister spoke and the choir sang, I thought about all I had learned in the past few days. I thought of how Sonja's cattiness, and Simone's bitterness, and Rolph's hyperbole had coalesced into portraits that might have been true likenesses of people, or might not. How tragedy could destroy a man like Ian Forrester, and loving care help raise him up again. I thought about the ways we, each of us, create our own truth and our own vision of reality.

The minister's voice droned to a halt. Zoe Outray stepped from the shelter of her husband's arm and dropped twin sprays of baby's breath onto her children's caskets. Then she turned and walked to the waiting limousine. A chauffeur tucked her carefully inside and closed the door. The other mourners wandered away in groups of three and four, their minds already moving ahead to Christmas dinner and midnight mass and presents under the tree.

Outside the cemetery gates, David was waiting for me. He looked younger than he had when I first met him. The lines of strain around eyes and mouth had eased. He smiled at me and I felt my step lighten as he reached for my hand.

Together we turned toward home.

ABOUT THE AUTHOR

Anne Metikosh has written a number of novels, short stories, and articles on a wide range of subjects. *Trial Run* is her first eBook and her first foray into romantic suspense.

She lives and works in Calgary, Alberta, where the magnificent landscape is her muse.

In the mood for more Crimson Romance? Check out *The Envelope* by R. Sue Oleson at *CrimsonRomance.com*.